DISH BEST SERVED COLD

LEIGHANN DOBBS
LISA FENWICK

1

Sarah adjusted her black chef's beret hat and tucked a strand of her long brown hair up under it in the back. She took a deep breath and looked around the large kitchen, pleased with how it looked. As usual, it was spotless, something that she insisted on. She liked everything in its place, and her staff knew that. The previous night had been hectic with an event, but one would never know it from how the kitchen looked now. The floors had already been polished and all of the rubber mats scrubbed clean, and the dozens of pots and pans hanging from the rows of racks were gleaming. All of the chef's cutlery was clean, the knives were sharpened, and everything hung in its appropriate place.

"What is that smell? It's amazing!"

Sarah smiled at Sue, one of the office workers at O'Rourke's Signature Events. Sue made her way down to the kitchen daily, regardless of whether there were events going on or not. She knew that Sarah was almost always experimenting in the kitchen and that she welcomed feedback. Sarah often placed food in one of the large refrigerators with a Try Me sign on top of the container, and the staff was always more than willing to help her out.

"Thanks. It's for the tasting tomorrow night. It's mashed cauliflower with garlic and rosemary. So many people are on low-carb diets, I figured I would add a spin on regular mashed potatoes, hoping that no one even realizes it's not potatoes! Try some."

She grabbed a large spoon and scooped out a mound for Sue, who eagerly grabbed the spoon from her and tasted it.

"Oh my God. You've done it again. I would have no idea that this wasn't mashed potatoes if you hadn't told me. How is this even possible? Amazing."

"Well, it did take me about three tries before I perfected it. I plan on serving sliced Kobe beef with it, and I didn't want the flavor to overpower the beef. Sometimes it takes forever to get the flavors just right, so that they aren't overwhelming. I don't want it to flop."

"Oh, it won't. Like always, it's perfect."

"Thanks. Tell whoever else is in that they are welcome to come have some. I'll place it in the usual spot, and they can warm it up in the microwave."

Sue thanked her again and left, and Sarah transferred the food into a large plastic container and put a sticky note on it. She would make a new batch tomorrow for the tasting. She never allowed day-old food to be served. Everything had to be fresh. Her kitchen, her rules.

After wiping her hands on a dish towel, she grabbed the top of the trash bag from the canister and pulled it out, twisting the top and tying it shut as she did so. She walked to the rear door and pushed it open with her hip. A few feet outside the door, she started to slide down the pavement, almost as if she were on a patch of ice. Except it was May, so slipping on ice was impossible. Her legs started to go in different directions, as if she were going to do a split, and her arms flailed around helplessly. Grabbing onto the trash bag with both arms tightly, she hugged it, thinking that if she fell forward, at least this would buffer her fall a bit.

She started to pick up speed down the ramp, the rubber soles on her clogs only making it worse when she attempted to pull her legs back together to try to stop sliding.

"*Heeelp!*" she cried out to no one in particular. She was alone, and aside from the kitchen staff and delivery people, no one was ever around back.

Finally, she was able to gain her balance when she was almost at the bottom of the walkway near the dumpster. Standing still for a minute, she tried to catch her breath. Then she slowly walked to the large dumpster, hurled the trash bag into it, and looked at the ground where she had slid.

Dang it! She had told her staff to make sure they were careful when they emptied the trash because the spills could be extremely slippery due to grease. Someone could easily break an arm or a leg, and when you were a chef, breaking either meant you were out of a job for a while. She walked over to the barrel that held sand in it, grabbed the giant scoop inside, and threw some sand down along the long slippery patch.

As she was throwing the final scoop down to cover the grease, she felt a chill, and the tiny hairs on the back of her neck stood up. She turned around quickly, as if someone was creeping up behind her. More than once lately, she had felt like someone was watching her, that something odd was going on. Just little things, like items being moved in the kitchen when she swore she hadn't moved them. Noises outside but no one else being there.

More than once she had wondered if maybe it was her ex, Raffe Washburn. Her relationship with him wasn't on the best terms at the moment. Working for him at his restaurant, EightyEight, hadn't worked out very well, because it wasn't working *with* him as she had hoped. It was *for* him. Something that she was reminded of on a daily basis when he would tell her that she took too long to plan the specials, or that a last-minute dish she had whipped up wasn't going onto the menu at all. Meanwhile, he was so slow and methodical with his planning that it led to the same boring food every day, and that wasn't what Sarah wanted to serve as head chef. She liked to be creative and different, spontaneous. That had been the whole reason that she had accepted the position in the first place, to have creative freedom. But having to get Raffe's approval days ahead of time wasn't exactly what she had in mind.

She sighed heavily, tossing the scoop back into the barrel and turning to go back inside. Thinking about Raffe made her sad, and she didn't have time to feel that way. She had a VIP tasting in less than twenty-four hours to focus on.

BRENDA STEPPED out a few feet from behind the dumpster with a smirk on her face. She could tell that Sarah was uneasy. She had looked around the area like she thought she was being followed. Good! She had looked funny sliding down, her arms thrashing around and legs going in different directions. Too bad she hadn't fallen and broken an ankle or a leg, though. If she had, then she wouldn't be able to cook, and that would have blown her chance for yet another article in which she was mentioned as being the head chef for the stupid big fundraiser that Gertie O'Rourke was having.

She kicked the side of the dumpster. Sarah didn't deserve any attention at all for being a good chef! She wasn't any better than Brenda had been during the Chef Masters Challenge in which they'd both competed.

BUT OF COURSE, because Sarah and Raffe were cheaters, *Sarah* got all the attention now. And it just happened to be a coincidence that Veronica, the assistant that Brenda had been suspicious of during the contest, worked at O'Rourke's?

That had basically sealed the deal that Veronica had been in on fixing the cooking contest as well, as far as Brenda was concerned. Heck, that old bat Gertie was probably the ringleader. Brenda knew they all played a role in getting her kicked off the show. Her cooking skills were too good. They had seen her as a threat and wanted her gone.

Meow!

She looked down at Kidney, Gertie's cat, who was rubbing up against her leg.

"Scram! Stupid cat."

The cat trotted away, disappearing into the thick brush that was up against the fence that ran along the property.

She eyeballed the cat. Anytime Gertie was in the local papers or on social media, that stupid cat was right there with her. Kidney! Talk about a dumb name. Apparently Gertie had come up with it because her long-lost daughter needed a kidney. Maybe, Brenda thought, she should mess with the cat. That would most likely upset Gertie more than if she burned the damn building down.

But Gertie wasn't the only person she wanted to make miserable.

Sarah, Veronica, Gertie…they all deserved to be taught a lesson. And, since they all worked together, it would be super easy to mess with them at the same time! But what else could she do? She really wanted to unplug some of the refrigerators and freezers and make the food spoil. But the doors were always locked, and the building was solid.

Aside from a vent that was on the side of the building. She had already unscrewed it and tried to stick her arm inside, but the vent was too long. She was pretty sure that the kitchen was on the other side of the vent, or at least close to it, because when she put her ear up to it, she could hear the faint sound of motors humming. What else needed to run all the time? If she knew where the plugs were, maybe she could snake a wire or something into the vent and yank the plugs out for some of the appliances. Or short-circuit them. Maybe she should do it at the last minute. It wasn't like they could repair an oven or the giant refrigerator last minute.

Her plotting was interrupted by a noise, and she quickly jumped back behind the dumpster and crouched down out of view. Slowly peeking out to the side, she saw Raffe Washburn walking toward the kitchen door. Good. Maybe Sarah would think that he put the grease there. Word on the street was that they'd broken up. Things with Sarah being the head chef at Raffe's super-trendy restaurant, Eighty-Eight, hadn't worked out as perfectly as they had hoped, apparently, because she was working for Gertie now. Boo-hoo.

Raffe hesitated at the bottom of the ramp that led to the rear door of the kitchen. What was all this sand doing all over the place? It looked like someone wanted to throw a beach-themed party. For all he knew, they were. They had some pretty crazy requests from clients, from what he had heard, and Gertie was known for being able to host the most extravagant events around.

He stepped around the mess and rang the buzzer, shifting uneasily on his feet while holding the bouquet of flowers that he had picked up away from his face. He'd never brought flowers to a woman before. He had had them delivered before, sure, but physically brought them himself? No. He had never really had to make much of an effort with any girlfriend. They always seemed to want to be with him all the time and hung on his every word. Except Sarah. She was independent and, well, different from all the others. She hadn't cared about his money and was very career oriented and a hard worker. Which was why he had thought giving her the position of Head Chef at his restaurant was a great idea.

She hadn't appreciated his feedback on her menus at EightyEight, but wasn't that what she wanted? It was his reputation on the line. After all, it was *his* restaurant. Sure, he wanted an eclectic menu, something different for everyone, but Sarah took so long to perfect her creations! He hated to admit it, but since she had left EightyEight, things had gone downhill. He wanted her back, at work and in his life. But it seemed like every time they talked, it ended up in an argument, and he hated that. Now he felt like he was walking on eggshells every time they spoke. He just wanted his girlfriend back.

"Oh... er... hi," Sarah said to him as she opened the door, looking irritated. She stepped outside and looked around the area and then back at him. "Have you been out here the whole time?"

"Uh, no. I just got here. I brought you these."

Raffe handed her the arrangement, the colorful flowers brushing against his head.

"Oh, uh… thanks," she mumbled, taking the bouquet and turning back to go into the kitchen.

Raffe felt awkward. Why did she make him feel this way lately? They had been so close before, and the conversation had been effortless. Now it was like pulling teeth to have a conversation. They were always short and tense.

"So, how's things going for the tasting tomorrow night? I bet you're whipping up some amazing food," he said, following her into the kitchen and feeling like a puppy dog.

"Yup."

"Uh, so are you free tonight? I thought maybe we could go out to dinner or to a movie?"

He watched as she took a deep breath. This couldn't be good.

"Sorry, I'll be here all night making sure I've got it all set for tomorrow. You of all people should know that I like the food to be spectacular. I mean, I'm still working on the side dishes, and I have no idea what dessert will be."

"You don't even have a dessert planned yet?"

As soon as the words were out of his mouth, he wished he hadn't said anything. She looked annoyed and rolled her eyes, which didn't surprise him. This pretty much summed up the last few months she had worked at EightyEight. How could she wait until the last minute to finalize the menu? At his restaurant, something like this would have been finalized at least four days ahead of time. Of course, Sarah had hated that. He should have just given her the flowers and kept his mouth shut. After several minutes of awkward silence, with Sarah ignoring him and puttering around the kitchen, he decided it was best to leave.

"Well, I'll let you get back to work. I'm going to drop by TJ's office for a quick visit," he said, looking at Sarah's back as she whisked away feverishly, not even turning around.

He walked by the flowers that she had tossed on the countertop. He shook his head as he left the kitchen area. Women! He just couldn't figure this one out.

2

Marly Kenney held up the tiny outfit, inspecting every inch of it. It had to be perfect for the charity ball. She measured the two tails that came down in the back of the tux. She had spent hours making this ridiculous little tuxedo.

"What is that? Is that for a baby?" Jasper asked as he entered her office, a frown forming on his face.

"No, it's for Kidney."

"Huh?"

Marly rolled her eyes.

"Jasper! Kidney, Gertie's cat? This is his special outfit for the charity ball this week, for the Kidney Foundation. Hello? We talked about this. Not to mention we are going to it!"

"Sorry, I forgot. As long as we aren't making baby clothes, I'm fine. You know how I feel about kids!"

Marly forced a smile as Jasper kissed her on the top of her head and left the room.

Yes, she sure did know how he felt about kids.

Raffe knocked on TJ's office door, which was partially open, and then stuck his head inside the office and looked around. His eyes fell to the small meeting table, where there was a picture of TJ and Veronica, taken at the beach. He knew because he had been the one that had taken it. TJ was Sarah's brother, and they were pretty close. Naturally Raffe and TJ had gotten pretty close when he and Sarah had been a couple, and it wasn't uncommon for them to double date. In fact, the four of them had done a lot of things together as a group. He smiled at the picture and the memory of that day at the beach with Sarah. The smile quickly turned into a frown, thinking about how things had gone so badly between them over the last few months.

His stomach growled, and he headed down the stairs and toward the lobby. It was lunchtime, and maybe he could catch TJ on his way out. He was starving and hated eating alone. Of course, he could always go eat at one of his restaurants, but that got tiring. He was there enough to work.

As he entered the lobby, he saw Edward Kenney at the front desk, talking to Myrtle. Edward's arms were moving around as if he were exasperated about something. As he walked closer, he heard Edward asking about Gertie, a question that Myrtle seemed to be ignoring as she continued to work on a crossword puzzle. The more Myrtle ignored Edward, the more animated his hand gestures became.

The phone rang, and she held her hand up to silence Edward as she answered it.

Raffe couldn't help but laugh. Poor Edward. It seemed that he was always trying to find Gertie, and it had never once dawned on him that maybe Gertie didn't want to be found. Everyone knew that she was dating Tanner Durcotte, including Edward. But Tanner had taken a consulting job in China that was almost nine months long, so to Edward, that must have meant that maybe he could work some magic and make Gertie change her mind and go out with him. He certainly deserved an A for effort.

"Myrtle, you look as beautiful as ever today," Raffe said. Myrtle smiled at him. "By any chance, do you know where TJ is?"

"Thank you, Raffe," Myrtle said, looking at Edward almost as if she were waiting for him to agree with Raffe's compliment. Instead, Edward was looking at his watch. Myrtle sighed, and Raffe couldn't help but wonder if she actually liked Edward. In a romantic way. They would make a pretty cute couple. Myrtle loved to travel, as she always talked about places she wanted to go. Edward always seemed to want to whisk Gertie away, but Gertie couldn't care less. At least that was what Raffe thought. "TJ went to run an errand with Veronica, I believe."

"Oh, okay. Well, I am starving and thirsty. Edward, care to go grab some food and a drink with me? We haven't talked in a while. It would be nice to catch up," Raffe said.

"Well, I was planning on staying here until Gertie came in," Edward said, looking toward the front door as if Gertie would magically appear for him.

"She's not coming in for a few more hours, Edward. I've told you that. She had errands. And after her errands, she has her daily call with *Tanner*." Myrtle rolled her eyes and shook her head, making the red and pink beads that were strung to her orange glasses sparkle as they caught the light.

"Well, that settles it. Come on, Edward, let's go so Myrtle can get some work done."

Raffe herded Edward toward the large glass door, winking at Myrtle as he did so.

"Myrtle looks really nice today, don't you think?" he asked Edward. It couldn't hurt to plant the seed, could it?

Edward scowled and paused, looking briefly over his shoulder at Myrtle, before he walked out the door.

"I didn't notice anything different about Myrtle. I hope I don't miss Gertie. It's been a few days since I've seen her. I don't want her to think I don't care about her."

"Edward, don't worry. I have a feeling that Gertie is really tied up with the VIP tasting and charity ball she's having. Better to just let her have some time, or else you'll get an eye roll like I did from Sarah."

The two men shook their heads in agreement as they walked outside. Women!

"Good grief, I thought he'd never leave!" Gertie exclaimed as she wheeled into the lobby. "For crying out loud, it's like I'm a prisoner in my own company.

I can't get business done with him always wanting to see me!"

She patted Kidney, who was sitting on her lap. That was his usual spot on most days, as Gertie and the cat had been practically inseparable ever since she had taken him in. Kidney had the run of O'Rourke's, with the exception of the kitchen and function rooms. He typically stayed in the lobby and office areas, where many employees kept treats for him. To say he was spoiled would be an understatement.

"Yes, Edward certainly is persistent," Myrtle said.

"Well, I'm going to go visit Noah. If anyone is looking for me, I should be back in two hours or so. Of course, the last time I was there, they decided to shut down visitations right as I arrived." Gertie frowned.

She had paid a lot of money to get Noah, her grandson, the best treatment available. The mental health facility he was at was top-notch, but they sure weren't very good with communication. Also, she didn't like how Noah had looked the last time she saw him. He had seemed wacky, like he was on drugs. Not street-type drugs—she knew he couldn't be on those, since they drug tested there—but the pharmaceutical type that just made him zone out and act like a zombie. That wasn't the plan the doctors had talked about with Gertie. She had emphasized as much therapy as possible and minimal medication.

"Have you talked to them again? About his treatment?"

"No, it seemed to fall on deaf ears the last time, and I didn't want to push things, in case it made it worse for him there somehow. It might be time to get him out of there. As soon as this ball is over, that will be my priority."

"Well, you always figure things out, so I know you will get to the bottom of things," Myrtle said.

"Was that Raffe that I saw with Eddie?" Gertie asked, fussing with Kidney's collar.

"It sure was."

"Hmm. He must have been here to see Sarah. I hope that's a good thing."

Myrtle nodded in agreement.

"Me too. They make such a cute couple! I do understand that maybe working together was too hard on the relationship, but now that she's here, maybe things have gotten better for them," Myrtle said.

"I'll stop by the kitchen later and talk to Sarah. I want her to be happy, after all. A happy chef is a good chef! And I need her to be able to make these charity events spectacular."

Kidney meowed loudly and jumped off of Gertie's lap, trotting toward the sun spot on the lobby floor and stretching out.

"It sounds like things are going smooth so far for the event," Myrtle said.

"So far so good! I even have Marly making a special custom tuxedo for Kidney, since he is the mascot for the event."

"How cute!"

Gertie smiled as she watched Kidney sunning himself on the lobby floor. Everything was going along as planned for the event, and she couldn't be happier. The charity was very dear to her heart, and it was important that it was a big success.

"Special delivery!"

Gertie and Myrtle looked over at the door to see Marly walking in with what appeared to be a shirt box.

"I wanted to get this to you for a fitting. I hope it's what you expected?"

Marley took the top of the box off and took out a small tuxedo jacket.

"That is so cute!" Gertie and Myrtle exclaimed at the same time.

"What do you think of the color? I figured black might be boring, and I wanted to tie it in with the National Kidney Foundation color, so we've got deep orange and black."

"Oh, what a great idea, Marly. This is perfect! Kidney, come here!" Gertie called the cat, who lifted his head up lazily from the floor and then laid it back down.

"This will do the trick," Myrtle said, reaching into her desk drawer. "Kidney, treat!"

The cat immediately got up and trotted over to Myrtle's desk then jumped up on it as she handed him the treat. She grabbed him and held onto him while Marly struggled to get the tuxedo on him. Kidney tossed and batted his paws as the tux was put on him but calmed down as Myrtle gave him a few more treats.

"It fits perfect!" Marly said, letting him down. He walked around the lobby slowly, as if trying to get used to the outfit, and then plopped himself down on the floor in the sunlight again.

"Do you think the tails are okay? I couldn't make them too long or else they would trip him," Marly asked, eyeballing the cat.

"I think it's perfect," Gertie said. "And look, he

doesn't even mind wearing it. This is a sign that the ball is going to be a big success!"

Sarah glanced over at the large bouquet of flowers while she sliced up a cucumber, the knife moving dangerously fast as it made the thin slices. Why would he bring flowers without a vase? Now she had to cut the flowers down, find a vase to put them in, and arrange them. Who had time for that? Not her. And why did he have to make that stupid comment about her not having the menu finalized? Hadn't he learned by now that she was spontaneous, and the main reason that she had left EightyEight was because he was the total opposite? Jeez.

"Wow, nice flowers!"

Sarah looked up to see Marly, who picked up the bouquet and smelled it before placing it back down.

"Are they for you?"

"Yup. From Raffe," Sarah said, rolling her eyes.

"Uh, they're beautiful. What's wrong?"

"Nothing. Well, I mean, wouldn't you rather get flowers in a vase? So that you didn't have to go get a vase and all that? I dunno. Maybe I am just being a witch because I'm stressed about this whole VIP tasting event and the ball. Nothing Raffe does lately makes me happy. It just annoys me!"

Marly laughed.

"I know the feeling. Jasper gets on my nerves a lot. You know that. It took a while for us to figure out how we could work in the same building without killing each other."

"Yeah, well, that's too late for Raffe and me. There's no way I will ever go back to EightyEight. That was just a nightmare. And pretty much what killed our relationship."

Sarah sighed, feeling sad. She hadn't ever really told Raffe that she wanted to end the relationship, just that she had wanted to leave EightyEight. And Raffe hadn't exactly said that he wanted to end their relationship, either, but after she had worked her last day at EightyEight, she hadn't heard from him. She didn't feel that she should have to reach out to him first, and it had just turned into a semi-childish game of waiting each other out. She had ended up being the first one to reach out but only because she had left some stuff at his place that she needed back.

"What are you doing here, anyway?" she asked, wanting to change the subject. Jasper and Marly had gone through some tough times, but things had been going good for them, both business-wise and in their relationship, and Sarah didn't want to be all negative Nelly about relationships to Marly. Since Jasper and Raffe were also friends, she didn't want Marly spilling any beans about Raffe that might make things worse either.

"I had to drop off the tuxedo I designed for Kidney."

The two friends looked at each other and burst into laughter.

"So last week you designed outfits for movie premieres for A-list celebrities, and this week it's a tuxedo for a cat. Cool," Sarah teased.

"He does look rather handsome in it," Marly joked.

"Oh, I'm sure he does. It *is* a cute idea. I shouldn't have laughed. It's just *so* Gertie's style. Go big or go home."

"Agreed. I need to get back to the office. Are we still on for dinner later?" Marly asked.

"Yes! I'm looking forward to it."

"Great. I'll see you then."

3

Raffe pulled open the heavy wooden door to Flanders and let Edward step inside ahead of him. Flanders was a small pub-style bar within walking distance from O'Rourke's that had become a favorite with the staff. The inside was casual, with a light-oak bar running the entire length of one side and the rest of the space consisting of pub-style round tables for four. The back held a small area where they had a musician set up on weekends, typically a one-man show with a guitar. The walls had various framed pictures of New York-based news headlines from the past. There was decent food, and the drinks were always strong. Raffe had spent many nights here with Sarah and TJ and Harper, one of the other O'Rourke employees.

He slid onto the stool across from the table Edward had sat down at and ordered them both a glass of scotch on the rocks from the waitress as she walked by. Whiskey wasn't something he usually drank, but he felt like maybe it would help ease his anxiety.

"So, what's new in your world? You're still pining for Gertie, I see?" he asked Edward.

Edward nodded.

"We just seem to have the worst timing. Whenever I'm at her office, she's never available. How can that be? She runs the darn place! And if I call her, I just get the runaround from Myrtle."

"Well, at least that means you don't get the death glare from her. Or whatever it is that Sarah gives me. She looks at me like I'm crazy for paying attention to her, or giving her something."

The waitress appeared and placed their drinks down in front of them, asking if they wanted any food, before she disappeared into the kitchen.

"Oh, I get the looks, believe me. When I actually see Gertie, that is."

Raffe grinned. It wasn't funny, but even with their age difference, the two men had the same issue. He had hoped that maybe Edward could give him some words of wisdom about women, but it seemed that neither one of them could figure women out.

"Maybe you should just sit in her office and wait for her? Insist on it, I mean, to get past Myrtle. Then again, there is that whole other thing," Raffe suggested. He wasn't too sure that Gertie was interested in Edward, but who knew for sure? Women were hard to read, and Gertie really was a busy woman, so maybe she just didn't pick up on the fact that Edward liked her.

"Other thing? What other thing?" Edward asked.

"Her boyfriend. Tanner. Edward, you know that just because he's been away for work, it doesn't mean that Gertie's single, right?"

"Pffft! A gentleman that really cared wouldn't leave his lady for almost a year! When I traveled, I always flew my wife out to see me every three weeks. Or I flew home. And as far as just waiting for her in her office, I've tried that, but Myrtle won't let me get past her desk! She's a tough one. It's like she's Gertie's bodyguard, for crying out loud. I could tell her that the building was on fire, and she wouldn't believe me at this point. I've used so many excuses to try to see Gertie. The president should hire her for a security detail!"

They both stared at their drinks for a few

minutes in silence. Raffe decided that he would drop the Tanner discussion. Edward was a stubborn man, and Raffe had enough on his hands with trying to figure out what to do to get back together with Sarah. Besides, he didn't really know the current status of Gertie's relationship.

"When I surprised Sarah with flowers earlier, she acted annoyed. Why would anyone be annoyed getting flowers? I mean, it wasn't like they were wilted or cheap ones either. They were an expensive bouquet of beautiful flowers, and she looked at them like they were a can of worms. The last I saw of them, they were sitting on the counter in the kitchen, not even in a vase. They'll die. Why would she just leave them lying there?"

"She didn't get a vase to put them in? There are dozens of them in storage there for all of the events! See, this is why I just don't understand women at all. I would love to receive a gift at work, or any time for that matter," Edward said in agreement. "Who doesn't like a surprise like that?"

Raffe shrugged as he watched a group of older women sit down at the table next to them.

"She complains that I'm not spontaneous enough, and then when I am, she gets mad. It just doesn't make sense. It's like what happened when she worked for me. I'd ask for her specials so I could put them on the menu, and holy cow, you would think I asked her to jump off the roof. Nothing was easy. It was like pulling teeth to get simple information."

The waitress returned with club sandwiches for each of them. Raffe grabbed the bottle of ketchup, placed a blob next to the giant steak-cut fries, and dipped one in.

"Maybe she doesn't like flowers. Or she could be allergic to them?" Edward asked.

"Doesn't every woman like flowers? She never acted like she didn't like them when we were together. And I know she's not allergic to them. I mean, she never mentioned being allergic to them," Raffe said. But maybe Edward was right, and all this time Sarah hated flowers? That would explain why she'd looked annoyed. But she'd always commented on certain arrangements at EightyEight and how pretty they were, and when they were together, Raffe had had a few bouquets delivered to her. She always thanked him and said she loved them. Why was this so hard?

"Well, what else can I bring her besides flowers? Chocolates aren't an option. She has access to so many and makes her own all the time. In fact, anything food related she probably won't like because she's so good at creating her own. And clothes are out of the question. I learned that lesson the hard way with another girlfriend years ago. I bought the wrong size, and wow, was that a huge mistake."

"Are you sure? I am kind of an expert with clothing, remember. I could make her a nice gown or dress," Edward said.

Raffe shook his head. Sarah wasn't a fancy woman. That was part of what had attracted him to her. She preferred to wear jeans or sweatpants, not glitzy gowns. Then again, she did try to get together with Marly a few times a month. Maybe a nice outfit for that would be a good gift?

"What about a puppy? No one can hate a puppy."

"She's not home enough to take care of a pet."

"What about a stuffed animal? You know, like a teddy bear with a heart or something?" Edward suggested.

The table of women next to them laughed, and Raffe looked over at them to see if they had been eavesdropping and were laughing at Edward's suggestion. The tables were pretty close to one another at the pub, so it wasn't hard to overhear what people were talking about. They all seemed to be looking at their menus, though. Great, now he was getting paranoid about this stupid gift!

"Hmm. You might be onto something! Who doesn't like a stuffed animal? It's not like you ever hear a woman say that they are ugly or that they hate them. And they always buy them for their kids!"

"Right? And you could get one of those really, really big ones. The bigger the better. That's what I always say," Edward said. "Also, you should put something on the bear. A present. Jewelry perhaps. Maybe a necklace around its neck."

Raffe shook his head.

"Sarah isn't really into jewelry. She can't wear any while cooking, so she just never wears it at all. I've bought her a necklace and a bracelet, and they just sat on her bureau."

They both watched the group of women next to them complain to the waitress that there was no room for their purses on the table and that the rounded stools didn't allow them to hang them on the back.

"I've got it! A purse!" Edward exclaimed.

Raffe perked up a bit.

"Yes! Women love purses. Sarah has a bunch of them. I think. And growing up, my mother had a closet full of them!"

"Oh yes. I know women who collect them. Every woman loves a great purse."

Raffe noticed two young women who were sitting two tables away from them giggling and shaking their heads. Were they laughing at his conversation with Edward about women? They were probably jealous over the purse idea.

"I'm sure it will all go fine. You are the best at what you do!"

Gertie smiled at Tanner's face on her iPad.

"Thank you, but you know how I get before an event. I just hope I get the donations I'm hoping for! Half a million dollars would help these folks out so much!"

"Well, you should be getting an envelope from my office today with my donation. I'm just sorry I can't be there in person to hand it to you, although I'm sure Edward is thrilled that I am not around."

They both laughed.

"You know Eddie is harmless. Besides, I'm hoping he writes a nice fat check!"

"Oh, I'm sure he will. Let's just hope there aren't any strings attached to it."

Gertie could tell by Tanner's tone that he was serious.

"Oh please. You know I don't have any interest in Edward! Don't be silly!"

"Okay, okay. I need to get my day started here. I'll check in tomorrow, okay? Love you."

"Love you too," Gertie said, ending the FaceTime call.

She looked over the paperwork for the VIP tasting for the third time. It was all in order, but she always had to triple-check. The VIP tasting was for a special group of people, kidney donors and recipients only. It was unfortunate that her daughter, Lily, couldn't attend. Lily was the whole reason that Gertie supported kidney donations, because without one, Lily would have died. But after her transplant, Lily had thrived, and she had met a wonderful man that she moved away to California with. Gertie had hoped that the two of them could have spent time together and bonded, but she was happy knowing that Lily was living a good life now.

Aside from that, she was thrilled that everyone had RSVP'd that they would attend, and she looked forward to giving them all a great time. The charity ball would be on a different day after the VIP tasting, and that was where she hoped to get a lot of donations for the Kidney Foundation. She had invited every friend and business owner that she knew and hoped they would all open their wallets to support her cause.

She looked out of her office window, across to the water. Her mind wandered to think of Noah. Her poor grandson. She had promised Lily that she would get Noah the help that he needed and told Lily to not worry about him, to live her new life. But Gertie had a feeling about the facility that she had placed Noah in. Something just seemed off. In fact, he was supposed to have been able to attend the events, but at the last minute, his counselor had called Gertie to say that it was probably best if he didn't come, that it was too soon for him to be around so many people.

Meow!

Kidney announced his presence, strutting over to the corner where he had a custom-made cat tree. He lay down on top of it and started cleaning his paws.

"Well, Kidney, I guess what will be will be, right? I'm going to go make sure Sarah's got all the food under control. I know the food is your favorite part!"

4

"Something in here sure smells wonderful."

Sarah placed the hot pan that held her most recent culinary creation on the countertop as Gertie rolled across the kitchen toward her.

"Good timing! Here, try a taste of this." She plated one of her appetizers, crisped scallops with a spicy honey sauce.

"Oh, that's so different! What is that sauce? Is that honey? It has a bit of a kick to it. Not too strong, though. I like it."

"Yes, do you think it's okay? I don't want it to overpower the scallops but wanted it to add to it. I had Marly try some, and she loved it." Sarah was always worried that her creative side was a bit too creative and welcomed honest feedback, which she knew Gertie would be sure to give. Last week she had tried making a new soup, and Gertie had said it tasted like dishwater. Sarah made a few adjustments with spices, and Gertie had loved it.

"Oh no, it's perfect! Just like everything else you make. Don't change a thing, dear. Is this for the tasting tomorrow or for the ball?"

Sarah smiled and grabbed a scallop for herself.

"Both. Since it's different people that are attending each event, I thought I would keep this on the menu for both events, as it seems to be a hit. Judging by the people who keep coming into the kitchen to get some, anyway."

"Excellent! So, not to change the subject, but I saw Raffe earlier out at the front desk. Are you two getting along better these days?"

Sarah frowned. She didn't really know what to say, but Gertie always gave great advice, and she knew she wouldn't judge her.

"Not really. I've been focusing on getting the menu for the VIP tasting and the ball ready for over a week now, so I'm sure he thinks I've been avoiding him on purpose, but I haven't. I've just needed to prioritize. He brought me those earlier." She nodded to the bouquet that was still lying on the end of the kitchen counter, the petals on some of the roses starting to wilt a bit from the heat in the kitchen and lack of water.

"Oh, how pretty! But where's the vase?" Gertie asked, looking around.

"Exactly. That's just it, Gertie. There was no vase. He just brought the flowers. Yes, it was a nice surprise, but I'm super busy trying to finalize foods for the VIP tasting tomorrow night, and having to cut the flowers down and find a vase for them isn't really what I want or should spend my time on right now. Tell me if I'm being a jerk. I'm sure I sound like a horrible person. I just don't have a lot of patience for him."

Gertie laughed and reached out and patted Sarah's hand.

"No, dear, you aren't being a jerk. Flowers are nice. But you bring a hand-held bouquet for when you're going to a house, you know, like if you were having dinner for him. Or when you're going to someone's house for the holidays. That way you are home and can easily grab a vase and then cut the flowers and arrange them."

"Exactly! Ugh, he makes me so irritated!"

"Go easy on him. Men can be kind of clueless when it comes to these things. They just think flowers are flowers. They don't think about if it matters whether they're in a vase already or not."

"I know, but it just gets to be so frustrating. I asked him to be more spontaneous, and I am sure he thought that's what he was doing when he just showed up with the flowers. It's the same as after I've worked a fourteen-hour day, and I'm all sweaty and gross and just want to shower and go to bed, and he thinks it's a good idea to go out to a late dinner. Why? I'm around food all day! After a long day, the last thing I want is to go out to eat. Isn't that kind of a no-brainer?"

Gertie laughed.

"I know just how you feel with that one. Edward is always asking me to go out to eat. I can do other things besides eat! Heck, take me up north, and we can go do some sightseeing. Just because I'm in a wheelchair doesn't mean I can't get around! I'm not a darn invalid!"

"Gertie, you definitely are not an invalid," Sarah said, smiling as she watched Gertie reach for another scallop, her bangle bracelets jingling as she did so.

"Are you interested in Edward? You know, as a boyfriend?" Sarah asked Gertie. She knew that Gertie and Tanner had dated after the kidney donation, but he had left for China or somewhere overseas months ago, and she never really heard Gertie talk about him.

"Eddie is a nice man, and it's nice when you have someone who pays so much attention to you…even if it is borderline obsessive."

They both laughed. Sarah knew she was joking. Everyone at O'Rourke's always joked about how Edward was like a piece of furniture in the lobby because he spent so much time there.

"But he's not really my type, and I have Tanner. He's been gone for a long time, I know, but we do talk almost every day, and this place keeps me busy. He makes me happy. Are you still interested in Raffe? Or are you happier being single?"

Sarah wasn't expecting that question and had to think.

"No. But I don't really want to be with anyone besides Raffe, and I'm not sure we can figure things out so that we can be together without constantly bickering. I kind of hoped that when I left Eighty-Eight to come and work here, well, that maybe things between us would get better. After he got over me quitting, I mean. But it's been a few months, and things just always seem to go bad between us. His schedule is more flexible than mine, but he always seems to ask me out when it's the worst time for me and isn't willing to change the day. And then that gets me mad, you know? That he's the one who can go out any day or time he wants but won't be flexible when I say I can't make a certain date. I guess maybe we are both a little stubborn."

"Ya think?" Gertie asked, laughing. "Like I said before, don't be too hard on him. Or yourself, for that matter. Sometimes people try much too hard on things that are fairly easy. Raffe is a good guy, and he's smart and handsome. He's quite a catch, from what I've heard. Just make sure you don't push him away for the wrong reasons, dear. Now, give me a scallop for Kidney. No sauce. You know how he loves seafood."

Sarah placed two scallops on a plate and handed it to Gertie.

With that, Gertie rolled out of the kitchen, leaving Sarah alone. She glanced over at the flowers again. Gertie had a point. Sighing heavily, she looked around for a vase.

"Do you and Jasper have any plans for dinner? I thought maybe we could all try that new Chinese restaurant that opened near you. I've heard that it's wonderful and that they have authentic Chinese, not this Americanized crap. My treat."

Marly looked up at Edward from her desk and smiled. He seemed so lonely lately. She knew he missed his wife, but over the past year, he had just seemed lonelier and needier than ever. Even though he still worked, he was really just needed for board meetings, which were only once a month, if that. He stopped by the office a few times a week and usually came by their townhouse on the weekend.

"I'm sorry. I have plans to meet Sarah. But Jasper would probably love to go with you. You know how much he loves Chinese. Maybe you could ask Raffe to go too. He and Jasper haven't hung out in a while."

"Oh, will Gertie be there with Sarah?" he asked, his face perking up.

"Oh no, sorry. It's just me and Sarah. We try to have dinner together as often as possible. Lately we've each been pretty busy, so it will be nice to be able to sit down and talk, instead of just seeing each other for a few minutes or exchanging texts."

"Oh. Yes, that's good. Keep your friendships when you're married. You don't want to be a lonely old man like me."

Marly felt so bad for him.

"Have you given any thought to that site I told you about?"

Edward made a face, and Marly knew what was coming up next.

"Oh God, no. No one wants to date an old man like me! Besides, even if they did, how do I know they aren't after my money? That's why I wish Gertie would realize we are perfect for each other. I don't need her money, and she doesn't need mine!"

Marly had tried to convince Edward to try online dating, or even to meet with a local matchmaker that specialized in matching senior citizens. He had refused.

"Edward, Gertie has a boyfriend. You know that. Just because Tanner has been gone for a while doesn't mean Gertie wants to replace him!"

"Nonsense! What kind of relationship can they have when he's spending most of the year in China?"

Marly sighed heavily. Edward was handsome, and yes, he was certainly rich. But he could be a real pain in the butt and stubborn at times, and *that* was why Gertie most likely hadn't been interested in pursuing a relationship with him a year ago when she was single. He just didn't seem to understand that, or if he did, he certainly didn't want to accept it.

"Okay. If you change your mind, let me know. I'm more than happy to set up your profile."

"Have a good night. I'm going to go hunt Jasper down."

Marly watched as he walked away, reaching in her desk drawer for some antacids. Her stomach was giving her issues again. She hoped it wouldn't act up during dinner.

5

Sarah stared at the can of shaving cream that was in the top drawer of her bathroom vanity. Although she had started out looking for a hair clip, she had ended up sitting on the edge of her bathtub instead, staring at the can for the last fifteen minutes. She and Raffe had never lived together, but he had spent enough time at her place to have had his own drawer in the vanity as well as space in her closet. She had thought that every trace of him was gone from her place.

"Grow up," she said to herself, standing up and closing the drawer. The one below it held her hair clips, and she reached for a black one. Twisting her hair in the back, she tossed it up onto her head, securing it with the clip. She frowned at her reflection and took the clip out. Her ash-blond shoulder-length hair fell down, the long layers framing her face. She dabbed a pink gloss on her lips and applied another coat of black mascara onto her lashes, making her blue eyes pop. She never wore makeup to work, and she had felt like getting made up to meet Marly out.

After a quick check in the full-length mirror that was on the back of her bathroom door, she adjusted her top, centering the V-neck. Satisfied, she reached for her wristlet on the table next to the front door and stepped outside, opting to walk to the restaurant as it was only a few blocks away.

Sarah nodded hello to the hostess at McKay's and walked toward the lounge area. She spotted Marly sitting in their usual spot at the end of the bar, her hand waving in the air as she talked on her cellphone.

She slid onto the black wooden barstool next to her and ordered a glass of white wine while Marly finished up her call. The lounge was fairly busy, mostly with people who had come after work to wind down.

"Sorry about that. As usual, there's an emergency at work. I wasn't sure what to order you for a drink, but I did order some soft pretzels and cheese dip. Is that okay? We can order meals after if you still want. I'm starving!" Marly said.

"That sounds perfect," Sarah replied, taking a sip of her wine and relaxing a bit.

"So, what's new? I feel like we haven't done this in forever," Marly said.

"Sadly, same old, same old for me. Things are crazy at work. You know the events that we are having for the Kidney Foundation are so important to Gertie, so she's been on top of everyone to make sure things are perfect. After you left today, she came in, and we had a talk about Raffe. You know how much she likes him. And as always, she gives good advice."

"The events are the talk of the town. We've made a few gowns for people. Edward made one for Gertie, and I don't think she even asked him to." The two women giggled. "So, how are things with Raffe anyway? Tell me if I should mind my own business. He's been going out with Jasper more than usual, so I think he's been lonely without you around. Between him and Edward, they're keeping Jasper busy."

Sarah sighed heavily before she answered Marly. Raffe and Jasper were very good friends, so the four of them had been together a lot while they were dating. Marly and Jasper were still together, and

Sarah did feel a bit like a failure when it came to her relationship with Raffe. She knew she shouldn't compare it to Marly and Jasper's, but it was hard not to.

"Things are the same, I guess. I miss him. But at the same time, I get so frustrated with him always having to plan things out, to never be spontaneous. I mean, we would go grocery shopping, and he would take twenty minutes just to pick out what kind of toilet paper we should get. Toilet paper! I don't know—maybe I'm just a grump, but between that and working for him, it just was too much."

The bartender placed two small plates in front of them, followed by the large soft pretzels and dip. The two women placed a few pretzels on their plates and eagerly scooped them into the warm cheese dip.

"I can totally understand what you mean. I honestly think the work situation was just too much. You're a very creative person, and Raffe said that's what he wanted. And then he kind of, I don't know, almost went back on his word? I mean, the food is great there, but it was the same dishes that all the other restaurants in the city have. Personally, I liked the food much better when it first opened up, when you created the meals and Raffe didn't really get involved much with the menu."

"It was definitely a letdown. I took it personally, which I know I shouldn't have. But he's just *so* methodical. He started to ask for menus weeks in advance and challenge my ingredients—'oh, you're using garlic? Usually we use pepper in that dish'—things like that. It just got so bad that I hated going to work. But I just quit my job. I didn't mean to quit the relationship too."

"Maybe you just needed some space? I'm pretty sure Raffe told Jasper that you guys weren't broken up for good."

Sarah wanted to ask more about what Raffe may have said to Jasper, but she also knew that maybe it was better if she didn't know. She already had mixed emotions over the whole situation.

"I guess we just need to sit down and actually talk things out like adults, but that won't happen until after the events are done. I suppose we were both a little too stubborn about the whole breakup—well, me leaving work—and then just not wanting to reach out to each other first. In the meantime, I guess I'll just be miserable second-guessing his every move."

The bartender approached them, and they both immediately said "yes" when asked if they wanted another drink.

"Well, you aren't the only one who is miserable. Lately Edward spends more time at our house than he does at his own. Moping around, talking about being lonely. I know he misses being married, having a wife. It's kind of depressing, to be honest. I wish I knew someone I could fix him up with, but I don't have any friends that are in their seventies!"

"He didn't go for the online dating thing, huh?"

"Nope. He thinks that whomever he would meet would be after him for his money. I tried to explain that there are matchmakers that he can sign up with who weed people out and can match him with someone who has their own money, but he didn't want to hear it."

"He's definitely a stubborn man," Sarah said.

"Ma'am, did you want Sprite or ginger ale with the cranberry?" the bartender asked Marly.

Sarah frowned.

"Vodka, soda, cranberry. Lemon, no lime," Sarah told the bartender, laughing. She knew what her best friend always drank.

"Sprite is fine, thanks," Marly replied softly.

"You're not drinking?" Sarah asked her, surprised. Not that Marly drank a lot. She didn't, and that was the point. She basically only drank when the two of them met up, or when she went to dinner with Jasper.

"I can't," Marly said.

"Why? Is everything okay?" Sarah asked, remembering that Marly had mentioned having a doctor's appointment a few days ago. "Oh God, what is it? Are you okay?" Her mind raced, worrying that Marly might have cancer like her mother had. They had talked about that before and knew that it was always in the back of Marly's mind.

"Everything's fine. It's just... I'm pregnant."

BRENDA PACED AROUND the tiny apartment as she talked on the phone to Dick. She hated living there, but it was all that she could afford for rent right now, especially since she wasn't working. Her full-time job was planning the demise of everyone who had gotten her kicked off of that *Chef Masters* cooking show. And it really was a full-time job, between following people around so she could learn their schedules and reading every social media site that talked about local events. She had learned a lot and was seriously considering becoming a private investigator when this was over. Maybe she would start her own company!

"Brenda, you can't live like this forever! Let it go! That chefs' contest was just a small blip of your life. Of *our* life. But it's all that you've focused on since it happened. You've let it take over your entire life. It's just not healthy."

"But don't you see that *we* should have won?" she asked Dick incredulously. How could he just be content with what had happened?

"Brenda! It doesn't matter! It was almost two years ago, and look what your obsession with it has done. We lost the restaurant, and we almost lost our house. Our marriage has suffered tremendously. This is insane."

She sat down on the old couch that she had bought on Craigslist for fifty dollars, the rickety springs sticking into her back through the flimsy brown fabric. They had lost the restaurant because instead of doing the marketing and managing the employees, she had focused on other things. Dick was right about that, and she felt bad. But she couldn't just let them get away with it! She was doing this as much for him as she was for herself. He just didn't realize that yet.

"I know you don't agree with me, but I'm doing it for both of us. You just don't see it. But you will."

"When? When will I see it? We are separated, Brenda. I'm asking you to please, for the last time, stop this obsession. It's unhealthy. We can get you some therapy, and then maybe we can work on getting our marriage back together. Please?"

Brenda sat in silence. She knew that no matter what she said, he wouldn't understand.

"I only need a few more days, and then we can talk about therapy. Okay?"

She didn't hear his answer, whatever it was. She was too busy thinking about what time she needed to get to O'Rourke's the next day.

6

The clock on the wall across from Sarah's desk ticked loudly, reminding her every second that she was supposed to be in the kitchen and not sitting at her desk.

She looked down at her phone and deleted the text she had written for the third time. Or was it the fourth? Whatever she wrote sounded so stupid!

She hadn't slept well at all. She had been too worried about her reaction to Marly telling her that she was pregnant. Or more like her lack of reaction. She knew that Marly had struggled for a year to get pregnant and that her doctor had told her that because of her endometriosis, she had a very slim chance of being able to conceive. The fact that she was pregnant was amazing, and Sarah should have jumped up and down and shouted from the rooftops in glee for her friend.

Instead she had choked on her drink and asked, "What?"

With the VIP tasting happening tonight, she didn't have time to go see Marly, and she knew that Marly was probably in business meetings all day anyway. She wanted to send a quick text to reassure her that she really was happy for her. Marly had confided that she hadn't told anyone else yet, including Jasper. This made Sarah feel even worse.

I'm so happy for you. You're going to make the best mom ever! I'm excited to be an aunt!

She hit Send and walked down to the lobby. It was time to focus on work. She had spent over an hour on that text!

"I've never seen you pace around like this. Is everything okay?"

Sarah nodded yes to Myrtle as she looked out the lobby doors for the third time.

"I'm just waiting for the final food for tonight to be dropped off, and I'm a little antsy over it."

Antsy was putting it mildly. She had called her supplier first thing that morning when she woke up at seven to ensure they would be dropping the beef off, but it was almost noon, and it wasn't there yet.

They started their deliveries at five, and she had assumed that they would have been at O'Rourke's around nine. Technically she didn't need it for a few more hours, but that would really be pushing it close to serving time, and she couldn't have that. Her anxiety was kicking into high gear.

"If they come in here for some strange reason—instead of the kitchen, I mean—can you let me know?"

"Of course, honey. If you need me to help with anything, let me know."

"Thanks, Myrtle."

Sarah headed back to the kitchen, hoping that the beef would arrive any minute so she could set her anxiety aside. She decided that she would have her usual pre-event meeting with the staff now, since things would be too busy later.

"Meeting!" she yelled as she entered the busy kitchen.

She had a group of a dozen or so employees that worked for her. Even though there weren't events every day, she always had the same kitchen staff. Gertie had agreed to it. They were paid as if they were full-time employees to ensure that they were always available. Every month the calendar filled up with more and more events, so most of them would be working a full forty or more hours anyway. Consistency was important in a kitchen.

"Okay, so I just want to go over things for tonight as well as emphasize again how important these next two events, the VIP tasting and the charity ball, are. Tonight's event is just a tasting. So, we have a lot of main dishes that are in appetizer portions. The menus and recipes that you need are right here. *Please* remember that this event is strictly for people who have either donated a kidney or received a kidney transplant, so there are special menus available for people with food restrictions. All the food will be labeled, along with the ingredients, so the guests can see them. The servers will be running the food upstairs, and I want to use the warming racks as much as possible so that the food is out of the kitchen and upstairs. We will also use chaffing dishes. Any questions on this?"

She looked around at the group, who all were listening intently.

"Okay, good. For the charity ball, we will have full courses. You've already been given the menu and recipes for this as well, but as always, I will probably have a few last-minute changes." The group laughed. They were accustomed to Sarah making last-minute changes and were able to handle them without skipping a beat.

"There will be light hors d'oeuvres passed around, with the main meal being seven courses. It will start with this soup, and since I don't want any catastrophes with serving soup, I'm using two giant pots to hold the soup in the rear of the ballroom, and it will be ladled individually up there."

"Will one of us be ladling it, or are you having the waitstaff do that?"

"I'm leaning toward waitstaff. I feel like I need all of you here, in the kitchen. How hard can ladling soup be?" Sarah asked, making them all laugh.

"Lastly, have any of you been dumping grease outside the back door here?"

They all shook their heads, looking at her in surprise.

"Why would we do that? We all know not to. Besides, a lot of us use that door to go in and out for a quick breath of fresh air. Slipping and falling on some grease and breaking an arm would suck," Jennifer replied as the other sous-chefs nodded their heads in agreement.

"Okay, I just wanted to check. Thanks, everyone." Sarah watched as the half dozen of them started to make their way to the appropriate section of the kitchen to start working on the food prep.

She walked to the door and stepped back outside, looking around and then down at the spot where the grease had been. She knew someone had to have put it there on purpose. Kidney whisked between her legs, running out toward the dumpster. She started to call his name and then stopped. They tried to keep Kidney inside ever since Gertie had adopted him, but it wasn't uncommon for him to bolt outside when he saw a chance. He always came back and usually sat outside the glass front doors, waiting for Myrtle to let him in.

She glanced down at her watch and looked around one last time. Still no delivery of the Kobe beef. It was one of the most important dishes that she had planned, and of course, today would be the one day that the delivery would be delayed for some —or no—reason.

"Busy, busy."

Sarah turned to see Gertie.

"Is everything going okay? The food is all set? All of your staff is here?" Gertie asked.

"Uh, yes, fine. It's all under control," Sarah said. She couldn't tell Gertie that the Kobe beef hadn't shown up yet. Gertie would flip a lid, and there was nothing worse than Gertie flipping a lid.

"Okay, good. Let me know if you need anything, dear."

Sarah watched Gertie roll away. Where was the damn beef?

BRENDA LET her breath out and stood up. Phew—that was a close one! When the cat had run over to where she was hiding behind the dumpster, she thought for sure that Sarah would have come chasing after it.

Meow!

Kidney rubbed against her ankle and started to purr, looking up at her with his emerald-green eyes.

"Go away, you pest!" she said, making a *pssst* noise at him to try to scare him away. Instead he sat down and hit her leg with his paw, looking up at her with his trusting eyes and meowing loudly, as if he were asking for her to pick him up.

She leaned over, lifted him up, and rubbed the soft fur behind his ears. The stupid cat sure was cuddly. Her heart softened as she held him.

Maybe she should get a cat. After all, she was pretty lonely, and having a cat around would be one way to make herself feel better when she was just sitting alone inside her cramped apartment. She got so bored sometimes. She couldn't afford cable TV, and watching the same few channels was so tedious. In fact, maybe she should just take this cat. He really seemed to like her. Plus, Gertie and all the others were extremely fond of him, so it would ruin their day if they thought he was lost. She had seen the cat riding on Gertie's lap in her wheelchair before when she was leaving at the end of the day. She bet Gertie would be devastated if she couldn't bring Kidney home anymore.

What was involved in taking care of a cat? "It can't be that hard to take care of you, right?" she whispered to Kidney, who purred in response. "A litter box, some catnip, maybe."

Her thoughts were interrupted by the sound of a truck approaching, the loud engine echoing throughout the otherwise silent area. She dropped Kidney, who let out an angry meow before skittering away into the nearby bushes.

She pulled the collar of her black chef's jacket up and adjusted the white chef's beret down low, so that it was almost below her eyebrows. She made sure that all of her hair was tucked up underneath it, and her giant sunglasses concealed most of her face. Not bad for a five-dollar purchase at the toy store. They were giant mirrored glasses that belonged to a police costume. They were perfect.

She reached down for the tote bag that she had with her, hesitating for a moment. Should she leave it here, behind the dumpster? She decided not to, as she didn't want anyone to steal it, and hitched it up onto her shoulder, trying to hide the bulk of it behind her back.

Just as the truck finished backing up to the loading dock, she darted out from behind the dumpster and marched over to the driver's side door. She knocked on it, looking up as she did so. The driver looked at her and rolled the window down.

"This needs to be dropped off on the other side, at the other loading dock," she said to the driver, pointing toward the other side of the building. She glanced at the kitchen door, hoping that no one would open it up. She had watched them receive deliveries before and knew that typically the driver got out of the truck and rang the bell.

"What? We always drop the food off here. It's the kitchen."

"Well, there's been a change. Unless you want us to use someone else who can follow directions, then

I suggest you just do what you're told. So drop it off on the other side, at the other dock. It's narrow, so you'll have to back it in. Just leave it outside the door. I have to go get a dolly to bring it in." She spoke gruffly, trying to sound like a man, which was probably why the driver was looking at her so strangely. Between her voice and the giant sunglasses, he was probably trying to figure out who the heck she was, but she didn't care. As long as that food didn't get delivered to the kitchen, she would be happy. No food, no party. Boo-hoo!

The driver rolled his window back up, shaking his head, and then proceeded to drive away.

She darted to the side of the building and skulked along the alleyway that led to the loading dock on the other side of the old mill, where the delivery would now be made. No one ever went over there, but just in case Sarah figured out that the food was there, Brenda wanted to see the look on her face.

She took off her sunglasses and chef's beret and settled down on top of a tree stump, reaching into her tote bag for the sandwich and water that she had packed. She thought she might be here for a while, so she may as well eat. It wasn't like she had anywhere else to be!

7

"It's a drizzle, from left to right. So, it's across the mozzarella slice diagonally. Watch, like this. Do it lightly, though, so not too much comes out. If you do it too heavy, it turns the whole mozzarella slice brown, and I don't want that. I like the dark line against the white of the cheese."

Sarah showed one of the sous-chefs what she meant, drizzling the balsamic glaze so that it made a deep-brown diagonal line across the slice of white mozzarella cheese. While she fully trusted the sous-chefs that worked under her, she was still a bit of a control freak when it came to presentation. Even though she had the same group of people work for her in the kitchen, most of the other staff also worked at another facility when there weren't functions at O'Rourke's. Sometimes she felt that they needed to remember that O'Rourke's was a five-star venue instead of just an average banquet hall.

When she was certain that he understood how to plate the mozzarella, she wiped her hands on her apron, looking around the kitchen and then at her watch. Still no food delivery, and the VIP tasting was only a few hours away. Her heart started to race a bit, and she ran through the food she had available to whip up another dish in case the beef didn't show up.

She walked over to the rear door and opened it up, hoping to see the delivery truck backing up to unload the food onto the dock. She jumped back a bit, startled, as Raffe was standing there instead of the truck. His arms were behind his back, as if he was holding something that he didn't want her to see.

"What are you doing here?" she asked him, annoyed and slightly suspicious. Why did he always seem to be lurking around, and why did he always show up when she was busy? It was like he had the worst timing ever.

"Uh, well, I'm being spontaneous. Surprise! And I came to give you this."

He brought his hands out from behind his back

to reveal a pink purse. A horrible, gaudy, very large pink purse with a gold chain strap. It had logos all over it, and Sarah knew it was a very expensive designer bag, but that didn't make it look any better to her. Everything was wrong about it. The color, the size, the style.

Sarah looked at it like it was a bug. A big, disgusting, pink bug.

"What is this? Why?" she asked him, not sure if she had heard him right. Why on earth would he be giving her a purse? Had she somehow mentioned to him that she needed one?

"It's for you." He held the purse out toward her enthusiastically, a smile on his face.

Sarah reached out for the purse, forcing a smile on her face and holding it out away from her body, like the purse was diseased. An ugly, diseased, bright-pink purse. What on earth was he thinking?

RAFFE WAS STARTING to get a headache. Why was Sarah looking at him like she was annoyed that he had showed up? Wasn't that being spontaneous, which was what she had said she wanted more of? And she hadn't liked the purse. She hadn't even faked liking it. He could tell that she had forced that smile and was holding the purse like it was contaminated with nuclear waste. He wished that he hadn't come at all. This was going horribly wrong.

"Raffe, when have you ever seen me carry a purse?"

Raffe thought for a few minutes while Sarah looked around outside impatiently, holding the purse by the strap with one finger. Come to think of it, he didn't remember her ever having a purse. She usually just had one of those small things that had a strap for the wrist. Her phone had a case that held credit cards and money. Was that all she carried with her most of the time? Ugh. He needed to remember to tell Edward this, that not all women loved purses. This was another screwup. An expensive one at that.

"Uh, I haven't, so… I… that's why I bought you this one. Because I thought maybe you needed a purse. To carry your stuff in." Raffe was lying, but she wouldn't know. He had to answer her somehow, and this was a pretty good one. She didn't have a purse, so he bought her one. That was thoughtful, wasn't it?

"Well, thanks. It's… this was… uh… thoughtful of you. I don't mean to be rude, but I'm running behind right now. I need to get all the food prepped for the

VIP tasting. By any chance, did you happen to see a delivery truck when you came down here, or maybe parked out front?"

Raffe could tell by her tone that she didn't want to talk to him anymore. So much for spontaneity. It was time for him to leave before this got any worse.

"No, I didn't see a truck. Or anyone else. Uh, I'll let you get back to work."

He turned around and started to walk slowly back to his car. So much for his big plan to wow her. The purse would probably end up with the flowers. Or maybe the flowers would be shoved into the purse and the whole thing thrown away.

"Are the clothes for the events at O'Rourke's all set?"

Marly took a deep breath, hoping it would help get rid of the nausea that was starting to bubble up from her belly.

"Yes. They were all delivered yesterday to whomever was on the list that Gertie had sent us."

Any other time, Marly would have explained that the custom-made gowns or tuxedos that Draconia had supplied to people for the VIP tasting were not on loan, that even though they were extremely expensive, the recipients were going to be given them. These people were donor recipients or the donors themselves, and many did not have the money to buy a fancy gown or tux just for one night. Gertie had insisted that she would pay, but Marly had insisted that she would not and that they would be gifts from Draconia.

"I'm hand delivering the ones for Gertie right after this meeting. They came out wonderful," Edward said, standing up and reaching for the two gowns that were hung on the mobile rack in the conference room.

Even though he was just a board member now at Draconia, Edward had insisted on designing the gowns for Gertie.

Marly's ears rang as the room full of people complimented Edward on the gowns. She started to feel woozy and grabbed the glass of water that was in front of her, hoping the cool drink would stop her nausea. Instead, she knocked the glass over, water spilling onto the top of the conference table as the people seated next to her grabbed their papers before they got soaked.

She pushed her chair away from the table and excused herself, jogging out of the room while she covered her mouth. As she ran past the employees on the way out, she caught Jasper's eye, his mouth wide open and a look of horror on his face.

Marly grabbed the paper towels, ran them under the cold water, then pressed them onto her face and neck. She looked at her reflection in the mirror and couldn't help but laugh at herself. Her mascara had smudged all over her eyes, and she looked like a racoon. She took a few deep breaths and stood up straight. She reached for the mouthwash and took a swig then swished it around in her mouth and spit it out. Thank God she had her own private bathroom in her office.

"Hon, are you okay?"

Marly's eyes opened wide. Jasper! Checking her reflection in the mirror, she wiped under her eyes and fluffed her hair a bit before opening the door.

"Yes, it must be something I ate last night. I'm fine, though, really. I already feel better."

"Are you sure?" Jasper asked, taking a step back from her. "What if it's contagious?"

Marly laughed. Jasper was a bit of a germaphobe and always ran in the opposite direction when anyone at work even sneezed.

"I'm fine. It isn't contagious. Don't be paranoid. Let's get back to the meeting. We're already behind."

She walked over to her desk and grabbed her

notebook, avoiding making eye contact with Jasper. Keeping her pregnancy from him was getting harder and harder. She knew she had to tell him that she was pregnant, but there never seemed to be a good time. Pretty soon she would start showing, and she would have no choice. What if he wasn't happy about it?

8

As she rummaged through her desk drawer, Sarah grew more irritated. Where was the sheet that had the contact information for the delivery company? The food needed to be here. Now. She needed to have it seasoned ahead of time and let it sit to absorb the flavors for at least an hour or else it wouldn't taste the same. Of all days for them to be late, why did it have to be today? She cursed herself for not having the contact info in her cell phone as she continued to look through her drawers.

"Hiya. I brought you some Dunks."

Harper stepped inside Sarah's office and placed the extra-large cup of iced coffee down on the desk and settled into one of the chairs across from Sarah.

"Thank you, I really need this!" Sarah exclaimed, happily taking the cup and a big sip of the ice-cold brew.

"I ran out for lunch and grabbed some coffees. If it's a bad time, I can leave. I'm sure you're swamped."

"No! It's a perfect time. I haven't taken a break all day, and I could use the caffeine. To be honest, I'm starting to freak out about the food delivery being late, and I need this distraction. So, what's new?"

"Eh, not much. Veronica and I have everything pretty much done for the events, so the time in between now and when they start is like the calm before the storm for us."

"How's Logan?" Sarah asked.

After solving the case at O'Rourke's last year, in which he discovered that Gertie's nephew had been trying to sabotage things, Logan had moved on to another case in his PI firm. Business was good for him. He had a few people working under him now and had established himself as the owner of one of the best private investigation firms in New York. Harper and Logan had been dating ever since meeting at O'Rourke's, and as far as Sarah knew, their relationship was still going pretty strong. Harper never talked about any drama or problems with him.

"He's good. Always working, you know how that goes. We fit in time to see each other between his stake-outs, which I guess is good because it's always quality time and we don't really argue. Last night I sat with him in his car for a few hours while he watched some warehouse. We had a little picnic in the car. It was kind of fun. He had this picnic basket and had gone to the deli and had it filled with sandwiches and some awesome pastries. How're things with Raffe? He just passed me outside. Are you guys still... err... on a break?"

Sarah stirred the coffee with her straw and then took another large gulp of the heavily caffeinated beverage. Harper got a car picnic, and she got a gross pink purse. Maybe she should tell Raffe to get some dating tips from Logan!

"Yes, we are still on a break. Or whatever it's called. But he did stop by earlier to give me this sweet gift."

She reached under her desk and slowly pulled out the purse, which she plopped dramatically on her desk in front of Harper.

"Ta-da!" she exclaimed, gesturing with her hands as if to show it off.

"Oh. Wow. That's... uhh... very... pink. And big," Harper stammered.

Sarah laughed.

"It sure is. And when have you ever seen me carry a purse? Or say that I like the color pink? It's so random and annoying. He stops by, interrupting me, to give me this hideous thing. Yesterday he brought me flowers but not in a vase. Just a big bouquet. It's almost like he wants to annoy me as much as possible, like he's trying to test my patience."

"At least he thought of you enough to go buy the purse and to try to surprise you with it. I mean, I know it's totally not your style, *but* it's the thought that counts. And let's face it, men can be kind of clueless when it comes to these things. For example, Logan got me a mop for my birthday. Besides, that's a Gucci, so even though he might be clueless on what to get you, at least he got you one of the best brands, instead of just grabbing anything."

Sarah felt bad. Maybe she was being too hard on Raffe. It was nice to know that he was trying to get her back, instead of just not hearing from him at all, or getting a late-night text every now and then like some of her friends did from their exes. She should probably be a little nicer to him, but this was happening at the worst time for her. Her attention needed to be on the charity events, not crappy gifts!

"Why was the food delivered to the loading dock on the opposite side of the building?"

Sarah and Harper turned to look at Veronica, who was standing in the doorway with her hands on her hips and a frown on her face.

"Huh?" Sarah asked, a pit in her stomach.

"The food delivery was placed on the wrong loading dock, the one way over on the side of the building that we don't use. Why did they leave it there? How long has it been there? What if it's rotted?"

Sarah jumped up from her seat, her heart racing.

"They know to go to the loading dock at the kitchen. Aside from being common sense, that's where they have delivered the food since day one."

"Well, not today," Veronica said curtly, turning on her heel.

Sarah exchanged worried glances with Harper, and the two of them followed Veronica to the other side of the building. She lifted up the large metal door, and sitting there was the food that she had been waiting for. She walked out onto the loading dock and looked around, knowing that she wasn't going to see anything. It was just an empty dark alleyway, the building on one side and a fence on the other. It was so narrow that she was surprised the truck had even been able to fit down it.

"Well, it's unfortunate that they dumped it off here, but at least it won't cause any major issues for the ball, right?" Harper asked, looking at the packaged meats.

Sarah opened up the box that was at the top of the stack and felt inside. Luckily the boxes were insulated, and since they hadn't been in the sun at all, the meat would be fine. It was still cool to the touch, and if anything, this may have helped bring it closer to room temperature, which was how she needed it to be prior to cooking it.

"It's fine, no risk at all. Thank God. I'll go grab a dolly to move these."

She went inside and grabbed a dolly, and the three of them started to load the boxes onto it.

"This is just really odd," Veronica said, placing a box on the dolly. "We get dozens of deliveries a week from Snyders, and this has never happened. Not even when we first opened up."

"I agree. I know it sounds weird, but I'm starting to think that someone is trying to screw things up," Sarah said. "What were you doing way over here anyway?" she asked Veronica. Why would Veronica need to be on the other side of the building? How would she know to open the door and see that the food was even out there? Like she had said, no one ever went to that dock.

"Why are you so snippy? Do you think I had something to do with this? I've been in meetings all day. Then as usual, Kidney was missing, so I went looking for him before Gertie freaked out. He likes to stalk mice in this alleyway, so that's why I was over here. Besides, if the food was so late, then why didn't you call the delivery people and ask them where the heck it was? It isn't like you to just sit around and wait patiently when it comes to getting the food ready for an event," Veronica demanded.

"Guys, calm down. I know everyone is under a lot of pressure for the charity events, but don't freak out. It isn't like someone did this on purpose. It was just a random mishap," Harper said.

"Yeah, I'm not so sure about that," Sarah blurted out. She wasn't sure that she should have said anything, but the tasting was only hours away, and she really had begun to wonder if someone was trying to screw things up for them. There were just too many strange things happening to be a coincidence."

"What do you mean?" Veronica and Harper asked in unison.

"Well, I don't know exactly. I mean, I don't have any actual proof. Some strange things have happened over the last few weeks, and I get this weird feeling at times, like someone's watching me. It hasn't been anything major, but they seem too odd to just be random."

"Strange things? Like what?" Harper asked.

"Well, like grease thrown all over the walkway that leads to the dumpster. I almost fell, and if I had, I could have easily broken an arm or a leg. It wasn't something that would have leaked from a trash bag being dragged out there either. There was a *lot* of it. And now this with the food. If Veronica hadn't found it, then odds are we wouldn't have had it at all for the event, and then what? It just seems like someone wants to ruin things."

"I don't know. Both of these things could be totally random," Veronica said. "Then again, who knows. It is a pretty high-profile event. Maybe it's someone with a grudge or something. But what kind of person would want to ruin a charity event?"

"That's a great question, but we better keep our eyes peeled. Just in case," Harper said.

BRENDA PEEKED out from behind the fence that ran alongside the alley by O'Rourke's. She rubbed Kidney between his ears as she craned her neck and tried to hear what the three women were saying as they looked at the boxes of beef sitting on the dock.

The look on Sarah's face had been pretty funny when she had first come outside and seen all of the food sitting on the dock. She had looked like she might cry. But if what Brenda was hearing was right, the meat wasn't spoiled, and it could still be used for the VIP tasting in a few hours. Brenda frowned and stopped rubbing Kidney, who let out a loud meow, leapt from her arms, and ran toward the women. She quickly stepped back behind the fence, mad at herself for yet another plan to ruin things that had gone wrong. She should have told the driver to deliver it somewhere else that wasn't even at the property, another venue. Time was running out, and so were her ideas. She needed to do something that would *really* mess with the event. Something that would bring it to a standstill and ruin the reputations of everyone who was a part of it.

Something big. But what?

GERTIE LOOKED out of her office window at the deep blue water. Kidney jumped onto her lap, and she started to pet him, a move that was automatic for her at this point.

"The water looks extra blue today, doesn't it?" she asked the cat, who purred in reply.

Something caught her eye, and she wheeled herself closer to the corner window, squinting as she tried to see more clearly. It was Veronica, Sarah, and Harper, all standing around something out on the loading dock that they never used. Gertie craned her neck, and as the women moved, she saw what looked like a food delivery being loaded onto a dolly.

What the heck was going on? Why would there be a delivery all the way over there? It wasn't even close to the kitchen. She watched as Sarah and Veronica lifted one of the heavy tubs together. At least they were getting along. She knew that Harper had most likely played referee more than once between them, and that was okay by her. They needed to let bygones be bygones. They'd be sisters-in-law someday if TJ ever got off his butt and proposed to Veronica.

Meow!

"Let's keep our fingers crossed that these events are a huge success, Kidney," she said to the cat, who jumped off of her lap, stretched out, and then trotted out the door.

Gertie sighed.

She really wanted to get as much as she could from the donors at the ball. The Kidney Foundation was so close to her heart ever since her daughter Lily had received a transplant, but also this ball could really put O'Rourke's on the map for hosting charity balls.

She looked over at a picture she had on her credenza and smiled faintly. It had been taken shortly after Lily got out of the hospital and was of Gertie, Lily, and Noah, right before Noah went into the facility to help his mental health. Gertie frowned. After Lily's operation, she had envisioned the three of them becoming a close-knit family, and that certainly hadn't happened.

Snap out of it, she told herself. This wasn't the time to start getting down about the past. She had more important things to do than feel sorry for herself. The VIP tasting was tonight, and she needed to check on the dishes that Sarah was working on.

She wheeled out of her office and down the hallway toward the lobby, where Myrtle was working on her usual crossword puzzle. There were hardly any visitors at O'Rourke's, so Myrtle really only helped answer the phones as well as with marketing and administration. She was extremely good at both and always had her projects done on time, if not early. Gertie didn't mind Myrtle working on crosswords at the office at all.

"What's a five-letter word for 'strips in a club' that begins with a B?" Myrtle asked.

"What? How would I know? You're the one that's the crossword expert around here. What kind of hint is that, anyway? Are those crosswords rated X?"

Myrtle tapped her pencil on the desk as she closed her eyes.

"Ha! I've got it. Bacon."

"Bacon?" Gertie asked. "In a club?"

"Yes. The club reference is to a club sandwich! You thought it meant a stripper pole, didn't you?" Myrtle asked Gertie, grinning.

"Guess I'm the one with the X-rated mind!" Gertie said.

They laughed as Gertie wheeled herself toward the elevator.

"I'll be in the kitchen if anyone's looking for me," she hollered over her shoulder. As she wheeled down the hallway, she decided to go the long way to the kitchen so she could check out the side loading dock where she had seen the women loading food onto a dolly from her window. She hit the button for the loading dock door, and as it slowly rolled up, she wheeled herself out onto the dock, looking around.

Meow.

Kidney bolted past her, jumping off the cement dock and darting into the bushes across the way.

"Kidney! Be careful!" she shouted after the cat, as if he could understand her.

Squinting her eyes, she rolled her wheelchair down to the end of the dock. Odd. There were clog prints in the dirt by the fence, small ones. Maybe a size six. Why would one of her chefs be messing around out here in the dirt?

9

"Myrtle, don't you dare shush me. These gowns are for Gertie, and I most certainly will *not* just leave them with you. They must be hand delivered!"

Raffe overheard Edward arguing with Myrtle as he entered the lobby.

"What's going on?" he asked, already guessing what the answer was. Edward had made two gowns for Gertie for the charity events. Not that Gertie had asked him to—he had taken it upon himself when she asked Jasper and Marly to make some for the event. Jasper had told Raffe all about it the other night.

"What's going on is that I need to get these gowns up to Gertie, and the gatekeeper here won't let me."

"Edward, I've told you ten times that Gertie left instructions for *me* to bring them up to her. *Me*. Not *you*," Myrtle said loudly, tapping a pen on her desk.

"Oh, can I see the gowns?" Raffe interjected, trying to lessen the thick tension.

Edward walked over to the rolling rack and lifted one of the gowns off of it, holding it up and cradling the lower part with his right arm so it wouldn't hit the floor.

"This is the one for tonight."

It was a beautiful periwinkle-blue off-the-shoulder gown that was fitted to the knees and then flared out a bit. There was an orange design that ran down the side of it, not too big, not gaudy, but very different.

"The orange is because that's the color for the National Kidney Foundation," Edward said matter-of-factly, placing the gown back on the rack and then removing the other gown. "And this one is the opposite in color, orange with the blue stripe. It's also more fitted at the bottom. I emphasized the orange for the second night, since that's when Gertie is hoping to really bring the money in."

"Oh, Edward, those are gorgeous!" Myrtle exclaimed as she stepped out from behind her desk. "They are so different. What are these, Swarovski?"

She pointed at the row of small crystal jewels that lined the top of each gown.

"Of course! You know Gertie doesn't like to wear jewelry. So I thought, why not just add it to the darn gown if she won't wear it!"

"What a great idea! And I love that you incorporated the color orange into them, Eddie. That's just so thoughtful. It's the same color in Kidney's tux. They'll match!"

"Thank you." Edward did a bow jokingly.

Was he blushing?

Raffe stepped back as he watched Myrtle and Edward interact, sensing a bit of chemistry instead of the usual arguing.

He walked away down the hallway toward the stairs. The kitchen was one floor down, the offices one floor up. Was Sarah in the kitchen or her office? Probably the kitchen. He pushed open the door that opened into the stairwell and almost knocked someone on the other side over.

"Watch it!" Sarah yelled as she jumped out of the way to avoid being hit from the door.

"Sorry, are you okay?" he asked. This wasn't exactly how he had planned on seeing her.

"What are you doing here?" she asked him, a noticeable tone of annoyance in her voice. Raffe immediately regretted coming to see her. "Why are you snooping around the stairway?"

"What? I wasn't snooping. I was on my way down to the kitchen to see you. I just wanted to wish you good luck for the tasting tonight. I…"

"Raffe, I'm super busy. I have one hundred fifty people coming here in a few hours and a million things to do!"

Raffe knew that the best thing for him to do was to just leave.

"Sorry, I'll go. I just…"

He didn't bother to finish his sentence, as Sarah was already on her way up the stairs.

SARAH STORMED INTO HER OFFICE. What was Raffe thinking, coming to see her today *again*? And right when she had to be getting all the food ready, which he, of all people, knew was when she did *not* want any disruptions! Wasn't the purse enough excitement for him for the day? Had he forgotten how to use his phone? Couldn't he just text her?

She grabbed the paper with the meat vendor's phone number on it and punched it into her phone.

"This is Sarah from O'Rourke's. Can you tell me

why your driver dropped the food off at the wrong loading dock today?"

She waited impatiently for an answer while she paced around her office. Even though the tasting was at seven and she really didn't even have time to call about this, the situation was bugging her, and she wanted to know why on earth they had put the delivery where they had. She tapped her foot impatiently while the receptionist placed her on hold.

"Ma'am? The driver said that one of your chefs instructed him to drop it there."

"What? Who? Did they get a name? What did they look like?"

She was placed on hold again, and Sarah immediately began to make a list in her head of who could have done it. Maybe it had been one of the newer sous-chefs, Amber. She was the only one who was fairly new, having only worked half a dozen events so far.

"Ma'am, he said he thinks it was a man with… some kind of big bag. Like a purse."

"What? He *thinks* it was a man? How can he not know whether it was a man or a woman?" Sarah questioned.

"Well, he said that the person had a very gruff voice and that they were wearing a black chef's coat and sounded mannish but also looked a little feminine. These days I guess that doesn't mean much. I'm sorry about the mishap."

Sarah's mouth hung open as she mumbled a thank-you and hung up. Raffe had been wearing a light black jacket that could have been mistaken for a chef's coat. And Raffe had had that stupid purse with him, and what other man around this place had a purse? Raffe wasn't really feminine, though, but she supposed anyone carrying a pink purse might seem feminine to the driver of the food truck. But why would he want to screw up her food delivery? Was this some kind of deranged plan to mess up her job at O'Rourke's so that she had no choice but to beg him for her job at EightyEight back?

She stood up and then sat back down, her mouth open. This couldn't be Raffe, the guy who had intentionally thrown the cooking contest that he had been so desperate to win so that someone who had less than him could win it. Raffe was a good guy. Wasn't he?

She didn't have time for this! She sent Raffe a quick text and hurried back to the kitchen. She would need to figure out who the mystery man or woman that had changed the delivery location was later on. Right now, she had one hundred and fifty meals to prepare!

"There's two? I thought there was only one. Oh, for crying out loud. I have one already for tomorrow's event, and I told Edward that ten times. Over there, see?"

Marly looked over at the gown that was hung up on a rack in the corner and shrugged at Gertie as Gertie reached out to touch one of the gowns that Edward had designed for her. She had no doubt that Gertie had told Edward that she already had a gown for the ball and that Edward had ignored her. He was a stubborn man and didn't change his mind often.

"I don't know what to tell you, other than you know how Edward is. Anyway, they did come out really beautiful, don't you think?"

She knew that Gertie hadn't even asked Edward to make the gowns in the first place and hoped that she wouldn't put up too much of a fuss over them. Even though Edward was a bit too much when it came to Gertie, Marly knew that he meant well. Plus, if Gertie didn't wear the gowns, then she knew she would have to listen to him whine about it for months, and she had enough on her plate to deal with.

"Yes, dear. I *do* like the color, the orange. It was thoughtful of him to do that. Except see here, the bottom of the blue one? That's a little too much fabric for me. It can get caught in my wheels. He forgets about that sometimes, that I'm in a wheelchair."

"None of us think of you as being in a wheelchair, Gertie. You run circles around us all! And we can hem that in easily. In fact, I can do it here, no big deal."

"Oh no, no. Just leave it as is, dear. I really do appreciate that he did this. But I will be wearing the one I purchased for the ball and this one tonight." She reached out for the blue one with the orange stripe. "I'm surprised that he didn't insist on bringing them up himself."

Marly laughed. "Oh, I'm sure he probably did. But when I came into the lobby, he and Myrtle were having an intense discussion, and I just grabbed the rack and said I would take them up to you, and he didn't object."

"An intense conversation?" Gertie asked, looking

up from the piles on her desk that she had started to look at.

"Uh, yes. At least it sounded that way. Something about Italy? Volcanoes?" Marly hoped she hadn't said something that she shouldn't have. It had actually looked like Edward was having an engaging conversation with Myrtle. His hand gestures were animated, and Myrtle was laughing. They hadn't even noticed her, which was odd for both of them, now that she thought of it.

"Italy! Well, good. Maybe Myrtle will take Eddie's focus off of me for a change."

Marly smiled. Maybe, and if so, that would be great. For everyone!

10

"Is this too much?" Brenda asked the salesgirl at the wig store, turning to her with the wig on. She had tried on a dozen wigs so far, and this one seemed to be exactly what she needed.

"Well, if you don't want to be recognized, it's a great option," the woman said. "Here, let me show you some that are less of a disguise type and more natural. We have—"

"No, that's okay," she interrupted the woman. "This is fine. I'll take it."

She paid for the wig in cash and left the store, humming to herself as she strolled down the sidewalk. This was perfect!

She noticed some people huddled in front of a window outside a store across the street and crossed over to see what they were looking at. It was a pet store, and she was looking down at the dozen or so kittens that were playing in a large pen. Maybe this was a sign, a sign for her to get a cat. She had thought about it a few times since being around Kidney, and why not? Cats were probably really easy to take care of, and she would love the company. Living alone was horrible, and if she did wind up back together with Dick, he would be okay with a cat.

She walked into the pet store and down to where more of the kittens were. She strolled slowly along the cages as the kittens played with one another, some of them reaching out of the cages and batting at her with their tiny little paws.

She peeked in at one kitten, and in return, it hissed at her, arching its back. She put her finger in to rub another one, and it batted its paws at her, trying to swat her away. None of them were as nice as Kidney, that was for sure. Were they all this nasty? Cats did have a reputation for being jerks. Maybe Kidney was one of a kind.

She heard a young boy around the corner begging his mother to buy a pet, telling her that they were on sale. On sale? Hmm. She walked over to the next aisle and saw a giant acrylic cage full of mice.

Dozens, if not hundreds, of them, running all over the cage. She made a face. She wasn't a huge fan of mice.

"Billy, we aren't getting a pet mouse! They are gross and carry diseases!" the little boy's mother said as she dragged him away.

Brenda stared at the mice and smiled. She had an idea. A really, really great one.

"We need more of those maple figs!"

"Got it. They'll be ready in five minutes!" Sarah said as she nodded to the server and scrambled to get more trays of the figs into the oven. They clearly were a big hit at the VIP tasting that was happening. She had messed around with the recipe, perfecting it only a mere hour before the event. Raffe would have had a heart attack. Maple caramelized figs topped with smoky bacon, the perfect combination of sweet and salty.

"Dear, we need more of the scallops! They're moving fast!"

Gertie's voice boomed throughout the busy kitchen, making Sarah wince. She knew Gertie made her staff nervous, and she didn't want them to be. Nervous chefs made mistakes.

"I'm on it, Gertie. A few more minutes in the oven, and they will be out. And the maple figs. Anything else needed? How's it going out there?"

"Very good so far. Everyone loves the food, so keep it coming. I can't wait to see what you have in store for the ball. And the entertainment has been wonderful. The only hiccup is that one of the servers had to leave for a family emergency, but Veronica has that under control as always. Overall, it's been an excellent evening so far. Keep up the good work, dear!"

Gertie had hired a swing band for the tasting, and from what the servers had been saying, the crowd loved the music. Sarah was relieved. The original plan had been for a comedian, but that had been canceled last minute, and she knew Gertie had scrambled to find a replacement. Everyone just wanted the VIP tasting and the ball to go as smoothly as possible. If Gertie was happy, then her employees were happy.

"Great, I'm thrilled that everyone loves the food. Go back out and have some fun. I've got things covered in here, but if you need anything, you know where to find me."

"Thank you, dear. I know you've got things covered. You know I like to keep everyone on their toes."

Gertie winked at Sarah and then wheeled away, the staff moving aside for her to pass through like the Red Sea being parted by Moses.

"CAN YOU START TOMORROW? We have a very important event we are staffing for O'Rourke's charity ball. It will just be serving food, helping to clear plates after, the usual function job. I have a girl there tonight that just had a family emergency and had to leave unexpectedly, so I'm really under the gun to get her replaced pronto. I promise we don't usually do this last minute, but we really need you."

Brenda smirked as the woman from the temp agency explained what she needed. Of course, Brenda had already known that they would be short-staffed. She had done her research and knew that this was the temp agency Gertie always used for her waitstaff. So, she had written up a resume, emphasizing her work at several banquet halls in another state, all of which were fake, of course. It didn't matter, because they wouldn't have time to call to check her references anyway. And when the woman she was meeting with had left for a moment to get some forms for Brenda to fill out, she had been able to pull a few of the resumes that were in the O'Rourke file for the temps that they used, basically ensuring that she would get a call for the next event. All it had taken was for her to call one of the girls that came from another state and tell her that there had been an accident back home and that her mother needed her right away. Brenda had started to feel bad lying about a family emergency, but it really wasn't hurting anyone.

"Oh, tomorrow is fine. It's perfect, actually," Brenda said. Perfect because she had one last errand to run, and now she could do it tomorrow morning, since she didn't need to be at O'Rourke's until late afternoon.

"Okay, great. The uniform will be at O'Rourke's, and if you have any questions, the other staff can help you."

Brenda hung up the phone and did a little dance. Things were going perfectly!

Raffe walked into the tavern and headed toward Edward, who was seated at the end of the bar, engrossed in a crossword puzzle. He sat down on the stool next to him and ordered a drink.

"I didn't know you liked crossword puzzles."

"Oh, hi. Thanks for coming," Edward said. "Yes, I love crosswords. They keep the brain on its toes! I try to do at least one a day, if not more."

"I was surprised when you called me. I assumed you were attending the VIP tasting tonight," Raffe said.

"I wasn't invited. It's okay, though. It's only for kidney donors and people who have received transplants. I'm going to the ball, of course. So, how are things with you? Did you surprise Sarah?" Edward asked him, still looking down at his crossword.

"Yes. And it was a huge flop. I guess I should have realized that she doesn't even carry a purse. So, that made me look like I didn't pay attention to things, of course. And then when I went by a while ago to apologize, I picked the worst time ever, and she practically kicked me out. So, needless to say, she wasn't exactly thrilled with me there. I blew it. Again."

Edward shook his head in disbelief.

"Maybe you should just tell her how you feel? All

these presents aren't doing much good. They seem to be making things worse, if anything."

"What?" Raffe asked.

Edward put his pencil down and looked at Raffe.

"Maybe we are overthinking this. Just tell her straight out how you feel. Maybe we both have been putting too much thought into physical things for these women and not enough thought into actually talking to them."

Raffe thought about it for a few minutes. It was pretty simple. Maybe Edward was right. Maybe he should just blurt it all out to Sarah. His phone went off, a text from Sarah asking to talk to him tomorrow morning at O'Rourke's. Was this a sign?

"Well, she just texted me asking to meet at O'Rourke's tomorrow, so I guess I'll find out how telling her straight-out works."

"Oh, tomorrow? Well, I will probably see you there. I drop by most mornings."

"You do? Why?" Raffe asked, already knowing the answer.

"Oh, just to see if Gertie wants to go to lunch later on, or to leave muffins for Gertie. But Myrtle usually shoos me away."

"Edward, do you think maybe Myrtle is shooing you away because Gertie's told her to?"

"Hmm, no, I don't think so," Edward replied, looking confused.

"Well, like you just said, maybe you should tell Gertie exactly how you feel. Instead of showing up every day."

Raffe sighed. Edward was oblivious to the fact that Gertie wasn't interested in seeing him.

"Do you and Myrtle ever chat about crossword puzzles?" Raffe tried to turn the conversation around to Myrtle. She was single and a bit sassy, which was the type Edward seemed to like, given his attraction to Gertie.

"What? No. Why would I?" Edward asked.

"Well, I've seen that she likes crossword puzzles like you do. And I'm assuming that when you're waiting for Gertie, Myrtle is the one who's keeping you busy, so I just wasn't sure if you two talked a lot. I'm pretty sure she loves to travel, and I know you do too. It just seems you have a lot in common."

"Well, we did have a good conversation earlier. When you were there, actually. But I don't think she's been told by Gertie not to let me go up to her office. That would be childish."

"What were you talking about? With Myrtle, I mean."

"Italy, of all things. She has quite the bucket list of

places to travel to. And some wonderful stories from places that she's already been to."

"It sounds like maybe you two *do* have a few things in common. She's an attractive woman, Edward."

"What? Well, I guess so. Yes. But I'm too old to be flitting back and forth with women. I don't think Gertie would appreciate it if I asked Myrtle out!"

Raffe shook his head and signaled to the bartender for another round of drinks for the two of them.

"Ten-letter word for annoyed and aggravated?" Edward asked out loud.

"Frustrated," Raffe replied.

11

Marly greeted the guests at the VIP tasting, stepping as far away from the food as she could. The smell turned her stomach, despite everyone around her praising how amazing it was.

"Thank you so much for the gown! I've never owned anything as nice as this before."

Marly smiled and made small talk with the guest, one of dozens that Draconia had designed an outfit for. She had agreed to come to the first hour of the tasting just to ensure that everyone's outfit was okay, as they had all been delivered only days prior to the event. Now she wished that she had sent someone else. Her stomach was churning nonstop, and the smell of the food made it worse.

"Do you feel okay?"

Marly turned to see Veronica standing there.

"Yes, why do you ask that?"

"Well, you're bone white, for starters," Veronica said. "Why don't you head out? I can handle things. Everyone that received clothes is here now anyway, so they should be fine. By the way, great job on the gowns and tuxedos. They all look beautiful. Including Kidney's!"

"Thanks. Yours came out amazing, if I do say so myself."

Marly had designed Veronica's gown herself, something that she never would have done willingly a few years ago. But Veronica was okay in her eyes. She had gone from being a trouble-making witch to a supportive friend.

Her gown was a beautiful plum color, lighter at the top and then darker toward the bottom. It was a one-shouldered style and fit Veronica's hourglass shape well. The once stick-thin woman had been self-conscious about her figure, and Marly had been happy that when Veronica had tried the gown on, it was extremely flattering.

"Thanks to you, it did," Veronica said.

"How's everyone? Did they all get their outfits?" Gertie asked anxiously as she wheeled up. Kidney was in her lap, looking like a tiny prince in his black-and-orange tuxedo.

"Yes, everyone got them. They all were very thankful. I'm glad we could do this for everyone," Marly said, wishing her stomach would stop flip-flopping.

"Everyone is having an amazing time, Gertie. I was just telling Marly that she should go home. We've got things covered from here."

"Yes, Marly dear, go home to Jasper. I am sure he would be happy to see you home so soon for once."

Marly forced a smile. Yes, Jasper would be thrilled to see her home so soon. Until she had to disappear into the bathroom.

SARAH LOOKED AROUND THE BALLROOM, impressed with the setup. Veronica and Harper really did know how to throw an event. The room had large round tables of ten for all of the guests, with a dance floor at the far end that was against a wall of windows that overlooked the water. Gertie had been given approval by the city to have giant spotlights shine on the water on the nights that there were events, and a gentle breeze rippled the water's surface. The large wall sconces had both white and pale-orange bulbs, casting a pretty glow up against the walls. The lights were typically a pale lavender but must have been changed to orange for these events.

There was a professional photographer taking photos throughout the event, and everyone was dressed in formal wear. The servers, who all wore white gloves, were passing around hors d'oeuvres and offering champagne and non-alcoholic mocktinis. There was a row of chaffing dishes that ran along the back of the room, and Sarah walked toward it, nodding hello to people as she walked by.

She checked each of the chaffing dishes, making sure that they were all full and that the food was warm. For the tasting there were several different dishes available, all of which were placed on each table. If people liked a dish and wanted more of it, they could find it in the chaffing dishes.

"It's all delicious," Harper said to her, accepting a bacon-wrapped scallop from a server.

"I just want to make sure it's perfect. They all seem to be having fun. Including Gertie," Sarah said, nodding her head to where Gertie was. Several people were standing around her, and all of them were laughing.

"It's a great group of people. There's some pretty

incredible stories too. Like, that guy over there? The super-tall one? He almost died, and then this guy over there, the one with the mustache, he donated a kidney to him. And guess what? It turns out they had gone to high school together and had absolutely hated each other. Mustache Guy had bullied Tall Guy. Now they're best friends."

"Wow," Sarah said. Harper always became a part of the event. She didn't just plan it, but she got to know the guests as well. She was a people person, and her name was always mentioned in the reviews that would come flooding in on social media after an event.

"So, the servers will start the main course soon. Followed by desserts. The food is all warm and ready to go, so you might want to get everyone seated shortly."

"Okay, thanks. Are you sticking around? You don't need to. The food is all set, and I know you've had a long day. I can call you if something urgent comes up."

"I'll be here. I just want to make sure the kitchen's cleaned and ready for tomorrow."

"I knew you would say that," Harper joked. "Try not to stay too late."

Once she was in the hallway, Sarah texted Raffe

and asked him if he could possibly stop by for a quick chat. Her earlier text had asked him to come by the next day, but he was usually working late at the restaurant. She had time now, and besides, she really wanted to know what the heck was going on. The whole delivery mix-up had really been bugging her—specifically what they had told her, that a man with a purse had told the driver to drop the food off at the wrong loading dock. She just needed to clean up the kitchen now, and cleaning was always how she fought through being upset. So at least if the talk didn't go well when Raffe showed up, she would already be cleaning!

"Desserts are in the refrigerated roll cases. Should we have them upstairs on standby and roll them in when food is done shortly?"

"Yes, please. Thanks," Sarah said to the servers. She took a deep breath. For the most part, everything was done for the event at this point. Everything needed from the kitchen, anyway.

"Everything's great. Gertie wanted me to tell you two thumbs up," Veronica told Sarah as she entered the kitchen. "And nothing seems to be off, you know, like anyone trying to screw things up. So, it looks like we were just being paranoid."

Sarah chuckled, smiling, thinking how there was

once a time she wouldn't have believed anything that came out of Veronica's mouth. Now the two were on good terms and worked well together to pull off the best events possible.

"I guess it's better to be paranoid than oblivious? And it's good to hear things are going well. That's great to hear. As long as everyone loves the food, I'm happy!"

"They are all raving about it. Especially how you have food for all the people on restricted diets because of their medical issues. Personally, I loved the scallops with spicy honey. Remind me to ask you for the recipe later."

"Scallops with spicy honey? That sounds good."

Sarah and Veronica turned to see Raffe standing there with a grin on his face.

"Well, I'm sure you can talk the chef into making you some," Veronica said coyly, winking at Sarah before she excused herself to go back to the event.

"Is now a good time? I was actually out eating dinner with Edward at Flanders when you texted, so it was easier for me to just swing by after we were done. I can come back later if that works better for you."

"No, now is perfect actually. Everything's pretty

much all set upstairs for food, so I'm just finishing things up here."

She walked over to the refrigerator, where she always had extra food, pulled out a small tray of the scallops, and placed them under the broiler.

"So, what's up? What did you want to talk about?" Raffe asked her, shifting nervously. "Is it about the surprise? If so…"

"Surprise? What surprise?" she asked, hoping that he hadn't left her another unwanted gift somewhere. She couldn't take it if he had. Her head would pop off from frustration.

"The purse."

"Oh, no. No, it isn't about the purse. It's about the food delivery. Did you tell the driver to drop the food off at the other loading dock?"

"What? What food delivery?"

"The Kobe beef for the party tonight was late. And it was because it was delivered to the wrong loading dock. They delivered it to the one over on the small alley."

"The one that you guys don't even use? And you think I told them to do that? Why would I even be giving directions to any of your vendors? I know I've been around here a lot lately, but I'm not an employee. I wouldn't do that unless you or Gertie asked me to."

Sarah stopped wiping down the stovetop and turned to look at him.

"Well, I called the vendor, and they said that a man with a purse redirected the driver to the side loading dock. And you're the only man around here that had a purse today. That I know of, anyway."

"Sarah, I didn't even see the truck. And they described a man carrying a pink purse? I mean, it wasn't like I was carrying it around like I had... uh... an actual purse. Okay, I guess when I walked from the parking lot to the outside rear door I was. But still, I don't have any idea why they would say that. I never saw any truck or even talked to anyone."

She turned back to the oven and pulled out the scallops, the tops crispy from the broiler. She reached for the bottle of spicy sauce, drizzled it on top of them, and then plated a few for Raffe. She pushed the plate toward him.

"They said it was a man that was a bit feminine carrying a large purse, or something like that. I mean, honestly, Raffe, I don't know why you would have told them to change the delivery location, either, but with the weird things going on around here, I..."

"Feminine? You think I'm feminine?" Raffe asked, seeming offended. "Me? How am I even remotely feminine? I mean, not that there's anything wrong with a guy being feminine. But me?"

Just then a loud noise came from behind the refrigerator, interrupting Sarah's train of thought. She walked over to the side of the fridge, and Kidney came strutting out from behind it with a mouse in his mouth, its long tail moving frantically back and forth out of the corner of Kidney's mouth.

"Oh my God! A mouse!" Raffe screeched and scrambled to hop up onto the counter while raising his legs up in the air.

"What the..." Sarah said, in shock at not just the sight of Kidney with the mouse but of Raffe jumping onto the counter and screaming like a teenage girl.

Suddenly dozens of white mice started to pour out from behind the refrigerator, scattering all over the kitchen floor like a white blanket.

"*NO!*" Raffe screeched.

Sarah shot him a look. This behavior was kind of feminine!

She grabbed the closest broom and swatted at the mice as Kidney scrambled all over the place, trying to grab a few more, his paws batting at them. Within a few minutes, they were gone, and Kidney disappeared behind the refrigerator. The kitchen was completely silent, the only noise being the distant beat of the band from the event upstairs.

"What the hell just happened? I don't believe this. This is nuts!" Sarah said, going to look behind the fridge.

"Help me move this out." She motioned with her arm to Raffe, who was still up on the counter.

"No way! Did you see how many mice there were? It was like a swarm!"

"Raffe! Get over here and help me! The mice are gone."

Raffe reluctantly hopped down and slowly walked over to Sarah, helping her push the large refrigerator away from the wall, exposing the wall behind it.

"What the heck? The vent cover is pushed so far out it's warped, so there's a big gap between the wall and the cover," Sarah said, getting down on her knees. She pushed with both hands against the cover, forcing it to bend back into place.

"That must be where Kidney went. It leads to outside, right?" Raffe asked, looking around behind him to make sure no mice crept up on him.

"Yup. Can you do me a favor and go outside and see what's going on? My guess is that the vent cover will be off the wall. If so, then the mice could just run right in."

Raffe's eyes darted around the room.

"Raffe! The mice are gone. You're fine. Check outside, please. Now!"

Raffe left, and Sarah looked around the kitchen. The mice couldn't have run off to the ballroom, which was where the event was. It was up several flights of stairs, and the hallways were brightly lit. Besides, the kitchen didn't have any open doors. There was just the rear door to the loading dock and the set of swinging doors to enter or leave the kitchen within the building. Most of the mice had seemed to run back under the fridge, so hopefully they were back outside. But she wasn't positive, and she couldn't risk any mice being inside the building. Gertie would flip out, and it wouldn't be good for business if customers started seeing mice!

"What the heck is going on in here? Did I hear a little girl scream? And why is the fridge pulled out, and why are you holding that broom like it's a weapon?"

Sarah cringed. The kitchen had been empty, and now Veronica was here because she had heard Raffe screaming. What if others had heard?

"We just had a mouse invasion. *Please* do *not* tell

Gertie! Or anyone else for that matter! Did they hear him scream?"

"Mice? What? Him—who? Wait—was that Raffe who screamed? Jeez, not very manly, huh?" Veronica started to laugh, and so did Sarah.

"Okay, but this is serious. I know it's an old mill, and I'm sure it was once full of mice, but we can't have this. I mean, I've never seen any up until now, no mice and no droppings. We keep this place spotless and have an A rating with the city inspections. I'll call an exterminator to be on the safe side, but we need to make sure Gertie doesn't find out about this."

"Agreed. The last thing that needs to be in the local news is that we are infested with mice! No one would want to have their event here, and we would all be out of a job," Veronica said.

Raffe appeared in the doorway.

"You were right. The vent outside was off of the wall, so there was a big hole. And it leads to behind the fridge. It's the exhaust duct. So that's how Kidney got in here as well as all of the mice. It's chilly at night, so they probably felt the warmth of the exhaust and ran right in. I screwed it back in, so we are all set for now."

"Well, there's one strange thing," Sarah said. "I

guess, in theory, that the vents could have just been damaged from usual wear and tear. And if so, I could see a few mice finding their way inside. But this was way more than a few. I mean, I'm not an expert, but I don't think mice run around in gangs."

"So, what are you saying?" Veronica asked.

The three of them all looked at each other.

"I'm saying that I think that this was done on purpose."

"What's going on?" Harper asked the trio as she entered the kitchen. "Raffe, was that you walking around in the alley?"

"Yes," Raffe said, looking at Sarah.

"We just had a bunch of mice running around in here," Sarah said.

"What? Mice?" Harper asked, looking around on the floor.

"Yes, I think they're all gone now. Kidney came out from behind the fridge with one in his mouth, and then all of a sudden, a ton of them started running out. The vent was bent open, and when Raffe checked the vent outside, it was open as well."

"There was a mice nest in the basement when I started here, and we had a really hard time getting rid of them. They had been here for a long time, it being an old mill. It was the perfect place because of the water nearby and the scraps of wood and stuff for them to make homes in. It sounds like maybe there's some living out in the alley area? I mean, there's the tall brush and the dumpster for food," Harper explained.

"That makes sense, then," Veronica said. "I'm going back upstairs before Gertie comes looking for us."

"You really think it's possible there're nests outside?" Sarah asked Harper, still doubtful.

"Absolutely. Trust me, there were a *lot* of them in the basement before. I'm going to go back upstairs as well."

Harper left, and Sarah looked over at Raffe, who was still looking around the kitchen floor as if he expected a mouse to zoom out at him any minute.

"Uh, do you want a scallop, or are you too afraid to eat now?" she asked, laughing.

He looked at her and laughed.

"Sorry. Yes, a scallop would be great. What a crazy thing to have happen."

"I agree," Sarah said as she plated some scallops for him. "I just hope that Harper was right."

12

Sarah grabbed the local copy of the weekly newspaper and hurried down the sidewalk on her way to work. She flipped open the paper and thumbed through, her pace slowing as she did so. She wanted to make sure that nothing about the mice had made it into the local gossip sites. She'd already checked social media, and so far, so good. Now, she just had to make sure it stayed that way.

She said a quick hello to Myrtle, who was busy writing some signage for the ball. Myrtle knew calligraphy and did most of the fancy writing that was needed at O'Rourke's. Once in the kitchen, she scooped some ice up and dumped it into her jumbo-sized coffee tumbler then slowly poured the extra-strong coffee into it. Adding what most people considered to be way too much sugar and a tiny amount of cream, she shook it up and then took a long drink from it as she leaned up against the counter in the kitchen.

She walked to the back door, looking at her watch. The exterminator was due any minute. She had asked him to park out back, next to the dumpster so that Gertie wouldn't see him if she were to show up early. She stood outside for a few minutes and then heard a car approaching. She turned to see the white van that belonged to the exterminator. He parked the van next to the dumpster and approached her.

"You Sarah?" he asked, extending his hand out for her to shake.

"Yes. Thanks for coming on such short notice. I really appreciate it," she said, walking him inside.

She went over all the details with him, explaining how the mice had seemed to pour out of the vent. He listened, made a few notes, and then said he would need to inspect the kitchen as well as other areas in the facility.

"Well, that's kind of an issue. I don't want the owner to know about this mice issue. I mean, you might find that it's not that bad or whatever, and I don't want her worrying about it."

He nodded his head in agreement.

"I understand. I can say I'm just doing an annual termite inspection if that makes it easier? If anyone asks, of course. I find that a lot of people don't really ask me what I'm doing."

"Hmm. That would work. Odds are you might not even run into anybody anyway. It's early, and our event isn't until much later on. Thanks," Sarah said.

"I'm going to go take a look around, but I want to place a few of these in some areas. Just in case. They are humane traps. The mouse will just be stuck inside this plastic thing."

He leaned down and placed one under the long counter island that ran in the middle of the kitchen and then went on his way to inspect the mill.

Sarah looked around the kitchen and paced a bit, unsure of what to do next. She had scrubbed the kitchen floor twice the previous night, with Raffe helping. Mice were dirty, and she didn't want any trace of them in her kitchen! She bent down slowly to take a peek in the trap that the exterminator had placed under the counter. She really hoped that all of the mice had left the building. Finding one in a trap would creep her out. And if Raffe found it, well, he would probably scream. She walked over to where she kept her files, pulled out the recipes for the evening's dishes, and started to review them for the last time.

"Well, this is just really strange."

Sarah turned to look at the exterminator, who was standing with his hat in one hand and scratching his head with the other.

"What's strange?" she asked.

"How many mice did you say you saw?"

"Dozens. Maybe hundreds. I don't know. They were all running so fast it was hard to tell. The floor was covered with them. It was like a blanket of mice."

"You're sure?"

"Of course I'm sure. Why?" Sarah asked, starting to get irritated.

"Well, for that many mice, there has to be a nest. There also would be signs, you know, like droppings or small holes in the walls. I've been all over this place, and there's none of that. Plus, I saw a cat roaming around. If there were mice here, odds are pretty high that cat would have run them all out."

Sarah frowned.

"What about that vent that I showed you? I know that's where they came from."

"Yes, I can see that, but it wouldn't make any

sense for dozens of mice to be together and just happen to jump up into that vent at the same time."

"This doesn't make any sense. I mean, I know there were tons of them. Small, white mice. All over the place. Moving together like a—"

"Hold on. Did you say white? They were all white mice? Not just a few?"

"Yes. They were all white. Not just a few of them, all of them. White with those beady pink eyes," Sarah said firmly. She was positive of that.

"Well, that explains it. Kind of. Field mice are brown. White mice are what you see sold in a pet store. There's some in the wild, but it's an anomaly, and certainly not in the amount you're talking about."

"So what does this mean, then?" Sarah asked.

"Lady, in my opinion, it means that someone released a bunch of pet mice in here on purpose."

BRENDA SAT IN HER CAR, with her giant black floppy hat and sunglasses on, and watched as the exterminator walked out of O'Rourke's. Ha! If only she had been able to see the look on their faces when all of those mice ran through the place last night. There had been too many people around for her to stay. It had been too risky for her to get caught, so she'd left as soon as she had gotten rid of the mice.

She'd been able to get a great price on a few dozen of them at the pet store, which had totally been a last-minute but brilliant idea. One of the quickest ways to get a bad review would be a mice infestation at an events hall!

The outside vent had been easy to unscrew, and she had just poured the mice into the opening. She hadn't counted on Kidney being outside and seeing her, but as soon as he'd seen the mice, he'd jumped inside the hole too. She had worried he would get stuck, but he didn't. Ha! A cat and mice running all over that stupid VIP tasting. Maybe the big ball would be canceled. After all, you couldn't have rodents all over a facility that served food. If the ball was shut down last minute, it would be in the news, and everyone would know.

She hoped that the news about this would hit soon. Thanks to social media, it would take no time at all to spread.

Something wasn't right, though. She looked around. The parking lot only had a few cars in it. Where were the news crews to report about the mice infestation? Why weren't there mobs of people there, taking pictures or hoping to get a glimpse of Gertie to put her under the gun to answer why she thought it was okay to have events when her place was full of gross mice? Actually, it looked like Gertie's van wasn't even there!

She saw the exterminator get into his van and scooted down in her seat so he couldn't see her. As she sat back up after he drove by, she saw Raffe and slid down again, her heart beating fast. If he saw her, it would definitely raise a red flag! Sitting back up after he drove by, she tapped the steering wheel with her nails. She needed something bigger that would draw some publicity. Bad publicity. Something that would shut this place down for good. Everything she had tried had somehow failed, only causing a minor inconvenience. She needed to step her game up. Fast.

"So, what did the exterminator say?" Raffe asked, looking around the kitchen. He was hungry and had hoped there would be leftovers. He really missed having Sarah's cooking available all the time. His house used to be filled with her recent food creations. Now it was just full of takeout boxes.

"He said that someone did it on purpose."

"Really?"

"They were white mice, which aren't wild mice. Those are brown. The white mice are what you get at a pet store, so he said it's most likely that someone set them loose in here on purpose. And that explains why there were so many all at the same time. He set up some humane traps, and I have a few for upstairs, but I don't think we need them up there. It's just a precaution, in case there are any that didn't find their way back outside last night."

Raffe looked around nervously. He really hated mice.

"Why would someone do that? Set a bunch of mice loose in here? I mean, what's the point?" Raffe asked, his eyes getting bigger as he watched Sarah take some food out of the walk-in.

"Do you want some?" she asked, taking off the plastic that was covering the large metal sheet. "It's just some of the hors d'ouveres. And the Kobe dish. Everything else is gone."

"That would be great."

He watched as Sarah put the food in the oven to warm it up, shifting on his feet a bit, feeling uneasy. He had decided that he would just tell her how he felt today, but getting the words out was harder than he thought it would be. He felt like a teenager again, unsure of how she would react, or if she even cared at this point.

"I'm not sure why someone would let a bunch of mice loose. It doesn't really make any sense. I mean, it isn't like Gertie has any enemies," Sarah explained as she flipped the broiler on to crisp up some of the food.

"Well, between that and the misdirected food delivery, it does seem like someone wants to screw things up around here," Raffe said.

"And don't forget about the grease that was thrown all over the walkway. You think they are all connected?" Sarah asked.

Now that she was saying it out loud, it did seem like maybe those were all targeted and on purpose. It was too much for a coincidence. But why?

"I don't know why, but I have an idea," Raffe said.

"I'm listening."

"I'll give Logan a call and see if he can set some cameras up quick, before the ball tomorrow night. That way we can see if anyone's screwing around. Odds are that if they are, ruining the ball was their main objective, and they still need to accomplish that!"

"Great idea. If he can possibly do it today, that would be…"

Sarah noticed a blur out of the corner of her eye and instinctively hurled a large pan at it. The loud banging noise made Raffe jump back.

"What the heck was that for?"

"I thought I saw a mouse," Sarah said, walking slowly toward the overturned pan.

Raffe stepped as far away from her as he could. She flipped the pan over. Nothing was underneath it.

Raffe let out a sigh of relief.

"Have I ever mentioned how much I hate mice?" he asked nervously.

13

Gertie waited impatiently in the hallway outside of the elevator, hoping that Edward would leave soon. She could hear his voice echoing throughout the lobby as well as Myrtle telling him that he should just come back tomorrow and that he would see Gertie then, at the ball.

Bang!

She heard a loud noise coming from the kitchen below. What could that have been? She crept closer to see if she could hear more, trying to stop her wheelchair from entering the lobby, but it was too late. Edward had spotted her. She had hoped to avoid him. He had been pestering her to go out for lunch today, but her mind and focus were on the ball, not going out. She sighed and continued to roll over to where Edward and Raffe were standing by Myrtle's desk.

"Myrtle, are you keeping these two out of trouble?" she asked.

"Gertie, you look stunning as always," Raffe said.

Myrtle winked at him. She liked Raffe. Hopefully he was there to visit Sarah.

"Thank you. I smell a new scent... Is that a new cologne one of you is wearing?" Gertie asked.

"Yes, it's me. I met with Sarah earlier and was just... uh... trying out some new cologne," Raffe explained, seeming to be embarrassed.

"Well, it smells wonderful. I'm sure Sarah thought the same." She really hoped that those two could work things out. She'd been thrilled when Sarah had called her about working for her but had felt bad that the reason was because she didn't want to work with Raffe anymore.

Edward cleared his throat, instantly irritating Gertie. She knew he was most likely doing it because he hadn't been addressed yet. She glanced down at his left hand, which was holding something. It was a crossword puzzle. Her mind started to race. Why hadn't she realized this before? Edward was lonely and loved to travel. Myrtle was lonely and loved to travel. Edward loved crosswords. Myrtle loved crosswords. Edward was a foodie. Myrtle was a foodie. This was brilliant!

"Eddie, what's that? A crossword? Looks like it's not finished. Have you asked the crossword expert for help?" Gertie asked.

Edward looked perplexed.

"Huh? Who is that?"

Gertie rolled her eyes.

"Well, it's Myrtle. For crying out loud, you mean to tell me that you're here almost every day, camping out at Myrtle's desk, and you've never noticed that she always has a crossword puzzle on her desk?"

Gertie glanced at Myrtle. Was she blushing? It was hard to tell with her bright-red eyeglass frames and matching beads.

"Well then, if you like to do crosswords, what's a four-letter word for Sicily Smoker?" he asked Myrtle, as if he were challenging her.

Gertie held her breath as she waited for Myrtle to answer. *Come on, you have to know this one*, she thought. *Show him up!*

"Etna!" Myrtle said, adjusting her eyeglasses as she did so.

Edward looked at her suspiciously then looked down at his crossword.

"How about that. You're right. I get it, Mount

Etna. The volcano, it smokes. Very good!" he exclaimed as he wrote the letters in.

"Mount Etna is on my bucket list," Myrtle said.

Gertie smiled as Myrtle went on to explain how she figured out it was Etna, and as she and Edward started to talk about how pretty Italy was, she decided that she had been somewhat successful in having Edward recognize that he and Myrtle shared a lot of the same hobbies. She headed toward the kitchen to see about that ruckus she'd heard.

"Oh, it was just a pan. It slipped through my fingers," Sarah explained to Gertie as she tried to subtly kick the mouse trap farther under the table with her foot. It was a small one made out of plastic, and it made a noise when she hit it with her sneaker.

"Oh, okay. It sounded like a bit more than that, but maybe it's my hearing," Gertie replied, looking around the kitchen. "I saw Raffe was here. Did you two patch things up?"

"Not quite yet. He was here to ask about the honey scallops. He loved them as much as everyone else did and wanted the recipe for his chef. I hope that's okay?" Sarah felt bad lying to Gertie, but she couldn't really tell her that Raffe had come by to see what the exterminator had said.

"Of course, dear," Gertie said. "So, how're things for the ball? Are you ready?"

"Good. Great, actually. Everything is all set. Is there anything you need me to do?" Sarah asked her.

"No, not unless you can make the dress that Edward made for me to wear disappear."

"Really? Edward's designs are usually really nice," Sarah said. He had designed a lot of gowns, and Sarah couldn't recall any of them being bad.

"Oh, it's a beautiful gown. But I don't want to encourage him. You know what I mean?" Gertie said. "In fact, I think he would be better with Myrtle. Don't you agree? I wonder what size she is. We're very close in shape. Maybe Edward's attentions would be better directed at her."

"Really? Myrtle?" Sarah asked. She had never thought about the fact that Myrtle might be lonely, never mind a potential girlfriend for Edward. But now that Gertie mentioned it, the two *did* have a lot in common, and Myrtle did always seem to take some pleasure in making Edward crazy when he was trying to see Gertie. Maybe that was Myrtle's way of flirting.

"Actually, Gertie, maybe you're right about

Myrtle and Edward. Good matchmaking. Maybe you should consider doing that. I've been meaning to ask about Noah. How is he doing?"

Gertie sighed heavily, and the smile faded from her lips.

"Oh, I don't know, dear. That place he's in, it gives me the willies. I just feel like something is off. It's hard to tell if he's really making any progress when he's doped up all the time."

"But it's one of the best in the country, isn't it?" Sarah asked. She knew that money hadn't been an issue when Gertie had been looking at mental health facilities. She just wanted the best for her grandson.

"Yes, it is. I can't put my finger on it, but I just get the sense that something isn't right there. You know I call every other day and visit as allowed. I just get a strange feeling. Oh, heck. I don't want to fill this place with negativity right now!" she said, throwing her arms up in the air. "Maybe a nice cocktail is in order."

Sarah looked at the clock on the wall over Gertie's head. It was only three o'clock.

"I know what you're thinking, but it's five o'clock somewhere!" Gertie joked.

Sarah grinned.

"Well, why don't you take the rest of the day off,

dear. Tomorrow's a big day, and I want you well rested."

"Are you sure? I was going to hang around in case anything came up." Sarah wasn't sure what could possibly come up, but she wanted to be there if something did.

"Don't be ridiculous. I'm telling everyone to go home early today, so just lock up and get a good night's sleep."

Sarah wished her a good day and was unbuttoning her chef's jacket just as Veronica and Harper walked into the kitchen.

"Wanna join us for some drinks?" Harper asked Sarah. "We can talk about... uh, talk."

Sarah knew that they didn't want to talk about the problem there anyway, just in case someone overheard and told Gertie.

"I sure do," she replied, reaching for her jacket and checking the rear door to make sure it was locked before she followed them out of the kitchen, shutting off the lights before she left.

"So, the exterminator is positive that someone planted the mice? That they basically bought them and set them loose at O'Rourke's?" Harper asked.

Sarah nodded, her mouth full of the chicken nachos that the trio had ordered. Flanders had great bar food. That was for sure.

"Yup. So, based on that and the other weird things that happened, Raffe dropped by earlier and mentioned that maybe he should call Logan and see if Logan can set up some cameras around the building. You know, just to see if anyone's messing around."

"Ahh, that's why he asked me what rooms would be empty. To set up the cameras," Harper said. "But what if Gertie sees him?"

"She won't. We can make sure of that. Besides, she's so busy with the events that she won't have time to be anywhere aside from the kitchen and the ballroom," Veronica said, loading some salt onto her sweet potato fries.

"Good point," Sarah said.

"So, Raffe seems to be popping by a lot lately, and now he's helping figure out what's going on. Have you two worked things out?" Veronica asked.

Sarah shrugged. "Kind of. We still have a way to go, but I think we will get there. We are both kind of stubborn, so it's taking forever to actually talk about the real issues, you know what I mean? Plus I've been busy focusing on the charity events."

"Well, I think it would be great if you got back together. TJ would love to have his BFF back."

Sarah laughed.

"So, if you get back together, will you go back to work at EightyEight?" Harper asked, her tone more serious.

Sarah hadn't really thought of that, and she could tell by the looks on Veronica's and Harper's faces that they wouldn't be too thrilled if she left.

"You've done so much for O'Rourke's," Veronica said. "And your staff loves you. As does the rest of the team."

"I know. I'm not sure what I would do about EightyEight if Raffe and I did get back together. I mean, just because we fix our relationship, I don't think it automatically means I want to go work for him again. At the same time, it was kind of my dream. To be the head chef at a five-star restaurant, I mean. Don't get me wrong. O'Rourke's is amazing, and I have so much flexibility. And I am beyond grateful to Gertie, and I really wouldn't feel right just leaving her to start all over again with a new chef."

"Maybe you could figure out a way to work at

both. You know, maybe you could create the recipes still for Gertie and work one day a week for the top event she has. Or you could do that for Raffe. Just an idea. You know she would die if you left. Plus, I don't want to have to try to find a replacement for you!" Veronica said.

"Actually, that's not a bad idea, working at both places. I really do love them both. Who knows what will happen? I guess anything is possible, and only time will tell."

14

Sarah rushed around the kitchen, triple-checking everything to make sure it was perfect for the ball. Her phone went off, and she glanced down at the text from Harper.

The cameras are all set up and good to go.

Good. That was one less thing to worry about. Raffe would be coming by any minute now to help them keep an eye on things.

"How much olive oil is in this?"

Sarah hurried over to her sous-chef to explain the recipe one last time. She had to weave herself in between serving staff that were at the front of the kitchen, most of whom were temporary help from the agency that Gertie used for events. Sarah always got a bit annoyed with them as they usually weren't familiar with the kitchen setup and just got in the way. That was why she tried to have food delivered directly upstairs to the ballroom and placed in warming ovens or chafing dishes if possible.

"Oh, I couldn't, Gertie. It's beautiful, but the one I'm wearing is fine. Isn't it?"

Gertie held her tongue as Myrtle twirled around in front of her in the office. Her gown was loud and garish. Like her eyeglasses and beads, it was bright and shiny, a red-sequined monstrosity in Gertie's eyes. Myrtle was a pretty woman, and her glasses often distracted from her beauty.

"Try it on for me, please. You know how Edward is, and he'll be so upset if I don't wear it, but I already have a gown I want to wear. If you wear it, maybe he won't be so upset. Plus, I think the color will look beautiful against your skin. You have a bit of a tan."

Gertie handed the gown to Myrtle, who walked over to the mirror and held it up under her chin, tilting her head and frowning.

"Veronica, come in here, dear," Gertie called out as Veronica passed by her office.

"Hi, Gertie, I'm super busy. Give me a few minutes, and let me just go—"

"What in the heck is that?" Gertie exclaimed as she wheeled herself into the hallway and pointed at what Veronica was holding.

There were two white mice in a plastic box that Veronica was holding as far away from her body as she could.

"Mice? Are those from here? Do we have mice? Oh no!"

"Uhh, no! No, of course not, Gertie. You know we keep this facility spotless. These are my... pets. Pet mice. You know, like hamsters? Mice are very smart. I bring them to work sometimes, just so they get out of the house and have a different view. I told you about them once, remember?"

Gertie side-eyed the mice, frowning as she did so. She didn't remember anyone telling her about having pet mice. She might be old, but she wasn't senile. And if anyone was going to have pet mice, Veronica would be the last person that Gertie would guess to have them. She was too uptight.

"Really, they are your pets? Mice, huh? Well, keep them safe from Kidney. He'd love to get his little paws on them."

"I will. By the way, I love his tuxedo for the ball! It's *so* cute!" Veronica gushed.

"Yes, it is, isn't it? I love how Marly was able to work the Kidney Foundation color into it. He's not the biggest fan of wearing it, but since he will get to eat his favorite food, those damn scallops, I think he'll be fine at the ball."

"Oh, he'll stay put for any food, that's for sure. Well, I need to get to my car. I forgot some toys for these guys."

Gertie watched Veronica walk away with her creepy pet mice. It sure was a strange choice for pets, but it was a sign of the times, she guessed.

She turned and wheeled back into her office, where Myrtle was standing with the gown on. It fit like a glove, and although Gertie knew Myrtle well, she certainly hadn't ever noticed that she had quite the hourglass figure. The length was perfect, and the flare at the bottom added a special effect to the gown.

"Not bad for an old broad, huh?" Myrtle laughed as she twirled around.

"That looks so amazing on you. You have to wear it! Here, let's do your makeup for you. We need a different colored lipstick and maybe less blush," Gertie said enthusiastically. Myrtle had a habit of wearing very bright lipstick and blush, and this dress and Edward needed a more subtle look for makeup. She was going to make sure that Edward noticed how great Myrtle looked if it killed her.

"Oh, that's okay. I know you are busy, and I am more than fine doing—"

"I insist, Myrtle," Gertie said firmly.

"Okay, okay," Myrtle replied as Gertie wheeled back into the hallway so Myrtle could get changed.

As she sat in the hallway, she thought about Veronica's pet mice. It just didn't seem right. And how she and Sarah and Harper had all been out on the old loading dock. Something was fishy.

15

"This glaze is so good. And broiling it to get that crunch is perfection. Really."

Sarah smiled as Raffe ate his third appetizer. The two of them were supposed to be prepping all the food, not eating it all! The charity ball was soon. Raffe had come by to help Logan set up the cameras and had stopped in to see Sarah.

"Thanks. I used spicy honey. We first used it at the Chef Masters Challenge, remember?" she asked him, placing a large sheet pan on the counter.

"Ahh, yes. So good. What's going in here?" he asked, pointing at the pan.

"Tomato slices with mozzarella on top. Then drizzled with balsamic."

Raffe frowned.

"What? Not good?" Sarah asked, spraying some olive oil on the sheet.

"Why don't you add something crispy for the top? You know, like..."

"Like this?" Sarah asked, holding out finely crushed panko breadcrumbs. They were homemade and had butter and a pinch of garlic in them. "I plan on warming them up in the convection oven so they are crispy and then crumbling them over the top prior to serving."

"Exactly. That's perfect!"

Sarah smiled.

"This reminds me of the contest. We worked together so well there. What happened? I mean... we didn't work like that at EightyEight. In fact, we worked the opposite way, more like we were on separate teams," Raffe said.

Sarah took a deep breath.

"I agree that we worked together really well for the contest. But when I started working for you at EightyEight, I just felt like you were micromanaging me. That you didn't trust me enough with the menu choices or specials, you know? And that really made me feel disappointed."

"I can understand that. And let me just say this

first, your food is always outstanding. It's just that you usually come up with the final recipe at the last minute, and I need some time to work them into the menu. You know we print the night's specials before one o'clock, but you don't usually have a final dish until close to five. So then it isn't in the menu or on the specials list, and it's up to the servers to remember to tell the customer about it."

Sarah stopped what she was doing. That example made perfect sense, but he had never actually told her that before.

"Why didn't you tell me that before? About the deadline, I mean?"

"I'm pretty sure I did. And let's not talk about all of the dishes you thought of last minute but didn't have enough ingredients on hand for, which meant we ran out after a certain amount had been served. Remember, people were starting to talk about the restaurant by saying that if you didn't get there before seven, the specials were gone? That wasn't the best publicity."

Sarah felt bad. She felt stupid and selfish. She had spent so much time focusing on Raffe asking her about her food that she hadn't stepped back and looked at the big picture of why he was doing it.

What restaurant wanted to run out of specials or not even have the item on the menu at all? Ugh.

"Welp, I feel like an idiot. I guess I owe you an apology for not taking the time to understand how my last-minute creations caused so many issues."

"You don't have to apologize. I should have explained things better, I guess."

"So, what could I have done to fix it?" she asked.

"Give me the details a day ahead of time. Or, if you can't, explain why, and maybe we could change how we do certain specials. You know, call it something else and have a special board for it at every table. Although I don't want the tables to be too crowded, so maybe that's not a good idea."

"Well, a day ahead of time doesn't really allow for me to be as creative as I want. No, not want. Need. I *need* to be creative."

"Well, maybe there's a happy medium. What about noon the day of? That way we have time to print the daily specials on paper as well as ensure we have enough ingredients on hand."

"Hmmmm…that could work," Sarah said.

"So, will you consider coming back then? To EightyEight?"

"Raffe, to be honest, I love working here for Gertie."

Raffe looked disappointed, and Sarah immediately felt bad.

"*But*...I do love having the ability to work at EightyEight and create specials. Is there a happy medium? I mean, let's face it. Maybe if I'm not there every day, it will be better for our relationship? I mean, if you still want one."

She realized that their talk had only focused on work and not their actual relationship. Maybe he only wanted his head chef back?

"Sarah! Of course I still want a relationship with you. I'm miserable without you. If you don't want to work at EightyEight, that's fine, as long as you're willing to give us another shot. That's all I care about. You."

Raffe moved closer to her, and just as he was about to kiss her, a loud noise from outside interrupted them.

"What the heck was that?" Raffe asked.

Sarah grabbed the closest thing she could, a meat tenderizer, and rushed toward the door.

"Stop! Don't go out there yet. We need to think this through. What if there is something—or someone—dangerous outside?"

It was too late. Sarah had heard him, but she was already halfway out the door, the meat tenderizer in the air. Something caught her eye, and she flew over to the dumpster.

"Aha!" she yelled, jumping out, her right arm raised in the air with the meat tenderizer.

"What? Oh, for Pete's sake, put that down, Sarah. What are you doing, trying to tenderize me?"

"Gertie! What the heck are you doing here?" Sarah lowered her arm, thankful that she hadn't whacked Gertie over the head. Maybe Raffe was right—maybe she needed to think about things before she jumped in.

"Gertie, what are you doing out here?"

"Looking for Kidney. I need to get him ready for the ball. He's the star! But I didn't see him inside, and I can't find him anywhere out here. I need to get back inside and find him before the ball starts!"

Sarah walked beside Gertie and opened the door for her. She watched her wheel away as Raffe stood beside her.

"Okay, so I guess I shouldn't have had such a knee-jerk reaction," she said, blushing as she went to put the meat tenderizer back.

"Ya think?" Raffe replied, laughing. "But in hindsight, we could have just looked at the cameras that Logan had set up to see who was out there."

Brenda rolled her eyes as she walked through the swinging doors back into the hallway from the ballroom. That idiot food critic Franz Durkin was at the event, talking to Veronica and Gertie in their fancy ballgowns. She hated Durkin because he'd been one of the judges at the Chef Masters Challenge.

The three of them were drinking champagne and laughing. Well, they wouldn't be laughing when their stomachs started to flip from the spoiled food. She stepped into the ladies' room to check that her wig was still on correctly. She hadn't worn one before and was worried that it would be crooked or fall off, but it was fine. A chin-length curly black bob and some thick, black-rimmed costume glasses, and she almost didn't recognize herself in the mirror.

She checked her pocket for the bottle of ipecac, patting it like it was a prized pet. It was concentrated, so a small amount was all that was needed to make a person sick to their stomach. She laughed, thinking how easy it was to buy it on the internet.

The bathroom door burst open, and a woman wearing a sky-blue gown flew past her into the end stall, where she started to throw up. Brenda made a face. Gross! Then she smiled, holding back a laugh.

It sounded like the food might already be bad. Maybe she didn't even need to go through with her plan!

Marly leaned up against the wall in the ladies' room, catching her breath. This was horrible. How come they called it morning sickness when hers was all day long? She took some toilet paper and wiped her forehead off then listened for the door to open. She felt like an idiot. Someone had been standing at the sink when she had run past.

She waited until she heard the door open and close before she left the stall. Running her hands under the cold water, she realized she didn't have her purse with her. She must have left it in Gertie's office earlier. She had shown up at the event early with Jasper and Edward. Luckily, her makeup looked okay. There was a knock on the door.

"Marly? Hon, are you okay?"

She stared at the door, knowing it was Jasper. *Yes, dear, I'm okay. I'm just pregnant*, she wanted to say. She had been putting off telling him because he had been so negative about kids lately. He was always commenting on how he was glad they didn't have any. He would point out noisy babies at restaurants or at the movies and say, "Thank God we don't have one of those."

How was she supposed to feel good about telling him that she was pregnant?

16

"Of course he's going to be happy! How can you think that he won't be?"

Marly's eyes welled up with tears, and she grabbed a paper towel and dabbed at the corners in an attempt to stop the flow.

"Ever since the doctor said that I might not even be able to have kids, he's been making comments. Just here and there, but still. What if he doesn't want to have kids?"

She took a deep breath and stood up straight. Maybe it was the hormones, but she had been overly sensitive the past few days. She really couldn't be falling apart right now, crying tonight at the ball.

"Marly, I'm sure he will be thrilled when he hears he's going to be a dad. You can't hide it from him forever! When are you going to tell him?" Sarah asked.

"I don't know. You're right. I can't hide it from him forever. And he's certainly going to pick up on it when I don't drink any alcohol tonight. As it is, I've been making up excuse after excuse over the last few weeks for why I've been sick or why I can't have wine at dinner. Maybe I will tell him tonight if the timing is right."

"I hate to tell you this, my friend, but odds are the timing will never be right."

Marly sighed. Sarah was right. Odds were pretty high that there was never going to be a good time to tell Jasper that she was pregnant.

17

Sarah wiped her hands on a kitchen towel, satisfied that things were under control. The main dishes had all been taken up to the ballroom. According to Veronica, everything was going perfect so far, and the guests all loved the appetizers. She told her sous-chefs that she needed to take a quick break and hustled down the hallway to the small room where Logan had set up the cameras.

"Any news?" she asked Logan and Raffe, who were both sitting in chairs across from the monitors, their eyes glued to the screens.

"So far, so good," Logan said. "By the way, nice job catching that perp by the dumpster. Tell me, was your plan to tenderize her to death?"

Sarah gave Logan a playful slap on the shoulder as Raffe laughed.

"I won't be quitting my day job to be a detective any time soon, I guess."

"Well, everything seems to be going as planned. Do you see anything or anyone who seems out of place?" Logan asked them both.

Sarah looked at all the different monitors, focusing on the ones that were in the ballroom, and examined the crowd of people. No one in particular stood out to her. It was all just the servers from the temp agency, a few members of her kitchen staff, and Veronica and Harper.

"Jeez, if there's a crime being committed, it's how bad Franz dances," Raffe joked, making Sarah and Logan laugh as they watched him on the monitor. He was on the dance floor by himself, spinning around in circles and clapping his hands.

"Wow, Myrtle looks fantastic!" Sarah said.

She watched as Myrtle walked past Edward to the dance floor and headed toward Franz. Edward did a double take as she walked by, looking her up and down as she slowly passed in front of him.

"Come on, Edward, ask her to dance!" Sarah heard Raffe mutter under his breath.

Instead, they all watched as Franz spun

Myrtle around. The two started to gracefully glide across the floor, with people moving aside as they did so. They waltzed across the dance floor and ended up in the middle at the end. The guests all clapped, and the two took a bow, laughing after they did so. Then the crowd started to leave the dance floor and head back to their tables.

"Hold on. What is that person doing?" Logan asked, zooming in on one of the servers, a woman with a small build.

"The one with the crazy curly hair?" Raffe asked, squinting.

The three of them all leaned forward, trying to get a closer look at the monitor.

"She's standing at the soups. We're having them served straight from the pot to the tables," Sarah said. "She's probably the one who is responsible for ladling the soup into the bowls."

Sarah watched as the server stood behind the table that held the giant pots of soup and looked around as if to see if anyone was watching her. Her mop of curls hung in front of most of her face, making Sarah cringe. What if some of that hair fell into the soup? Servers were supposed to have their hair pulled back! As if she heard what Sarah was thinking, the woman pushed the curls off of her face, causing Raffe and Sarah to gasp.

"Brenda?" they asked in unison, turning to look at each other.

"You know her?" Logan asked.

"Yes, she was in the Chef Masters cooking contest. And she didn't like us very much," Sarah explained. "This can't be good. In fact, this could be really, really, bad. We—"

"Let's go *now*!" Raffe had jumped up from his chair and was already halfway out the door.

"Raffe! What about a plan? Are we just going to run in there?" Sarah shouted after him, with Logan following right behind her.

"Sometimes it's good to be spontaneous!" Raffe said, pausing only long enough to grab her hand and pull her after him.

BRENDA SMILED IN TRIUMPH. Everyone was seated, and any minute now, she would be cheerfully serving each and every one of them a nice bowl of soup with enough ipecac to bring them to their knees. She couldn't wait until the entire ballroom floor was covered with people sick to their stomachs, including that idiot food critic Franz. That certainly wouldn't be a five-star review!

"One bowl, please."

Brenda faked a smile, grabbed the ladle, and scooped up some soup, pouring it into the bowl set strategically behind the giant soup pots. No one saw her add the drops of ipecac from behind it. It took seconds, and she handed the bowl to the server with a big smile. *So it begins!*

"LADIES AND GENTLEMEN, I wanted to thank you all for coming. As you all know, the Kidney Foundation is very near and dear to my heart, and I thank you for coming to help me continue to support this great cause. To start our night off, our mascot, Kidney, will taste the first bowl of soup!"

Brenda froze. What? No! Why would they be giving soup to a cat, for crying out loud! The ipecac... Kidney couldn't eat that. He could die! She couldn't bear the thought of killing Kidney. That stupid cat had been the only thing that had shown her affection over the last few weeks. She needed to protect him.

"*Noooo!*" she screamed, dashing out from behind the table and running onto the dance floor, where Gertie was with Kidney beside her. Brenda knocked the bowl of soup out of Gertie's hand, causing Kidney to meow loudly and jump out of the way of the falling bowl. The startled cat ran into the crowd of people that were watching with their mouths open.

"Oh, God," a voice said, and everyone turned to look at Marly, who was seated at one of the tables directly in front of the dance floor. Everyone ewwed as she threw up into her napkin, aside from Jasper, who had jumped up and was holding a large cloth napkin in front of her as if to shield her from view.

"Gertie!" Sarah screamed as she dashed toward Gertie, worried that she may have been burnt by the hot soup that was now all over the floor.

"You all know I like to make a splash!" Gertie said, laughing as she reached an arm out toward Sarah. "Please, bear with me just a moment."

"Are you okay?" Sarah asked Gertie as she looked over toward the side of the room. Logan and Raffe had grabbed Brenda and were heading toward the door with her.

"Yes, for crying out loud. What in the heck is going on? I have guests here! Who was that crazy woman, and why did she knock that bowl out of my hands?"

"That was Brenda. Crazy Brenda from the Chef Masters cooking contest. I think she's been trying to sabotage this event for a while now, Gertie. I'm not sure what the whole story is, but Raffe and Logan will find out. They've got it under control."

She watched Logan and Raffe as they pulled Brenda outside the doors so that she wasn't inside the ballroom anymore. Someone ran to the dance floor and cleaned up the soup that had spilled onto the floor.

"You can go ahead and talk again. We'll get the soup served," Sarah said to Gertie, who was already pulling the microphone up to her mouth to kick off the dinner.

Sarah ran over to the door and swung it open then stepped out into the hallway to see Brenda sitting in a chair and Raffe and Logan standing in front of her.

"What's going on? Why are you here?" she asked Brenda.

"She was trying to ruin the event. Look what we found in her pocket," Raffe said as Logan held up the bottle of ipecac.

"What? People would throw up if they had this.

Why would you want to make everyone sick? Is it because of the cooking contest?"

"I'm sorry," Brenda said, starting to cry. "I just—I couldn't take it. I'm a great cook! And I needed that money to help save my restaurant!"

"So, you decided to try to destroy Gertie's? As well as my reputation? I mean, if everyone threw up, then it would look like I cooked up a bunch of bad food, right?"

Brenda nodded. "I didn't want to hurt anyone. I swear! And as soon as I saw that Kidney would be the first to eat the soup, I knew I was wrong. That's why I ran out and knocked the bowl away from Gertie! I couldn't bear to think about Kidney being hurt!"

"So, I assume it was you that did the other strange things around here, too? The mice, the grease, the delivery at the wrong loading dock?"

Brenda nodded and hung her head.

"The ipecac only made it into one bowl of soup."

"Oh my God," Sarah said, running toward the ballroom again.

"What's wrong?" Raffe asked.

"Marly! She threw up! She must have had some of the ipecac!"

"I wasn't poisoned," Marly said, opening her eyes wide and nodding her head slightly at Jasper. Had Sarah forgotten? Jasper was right next to her, so it wasn't like she could say why she had thrown up. It had nothing to do with anything crazy Brenda did.

"Honey, how do you know? That woman is crazy. I think we should have you checked out, just to be sure. I mean, you *did* throw up," Jasper said.

"I'm fine," Marly said sternly.

"Dear, I think Jasper has a good point. Let's get you checked out, just in case," Gertie chimed in.

Marly threw a dirty look at Sarah, whose eyes were wide open now, as if she realized she had made a mistake by bringing this up in the first place.

"I wasn't poisoned," Marly repeated, frustrated.

"How can you be so sure?" Veronica asked.

"Because it wasn't poison that made me throw up."

"But we need to make sure. We—"

"I. Am. Pregnant."

The room grew quiet, aside from Jasper dropping his glass on the floor.

"What?" he asked.

Sarah nodded to the others, and they all crept away, leaving Marly and Jasper alone.

"I'm pregnant," Marly said, starting to cry.

Jasper hugged her, pulling back.

"Why are you crying? How long have you known? Why didn't you tell me?"

"I didn't tell you because you hate kids," she said, suddenly feeling a bit better. The wave of nausea had passed.

"What? Why do you think I hate kids?" Jasper asked.

"Well, all you do is make negative comments about them. Any time we see kids when we are out, or if a baby commercial comes on. It seems to be nonstop. Maybe it's just me. I'm overly sensitive, I guess," she said, feeling bad.

"No, you're right. I have been going out of my way to act like I don't want kids ever since the doctor told you last year that you might not be able to have them. I just wanted to try to make it seem like it wouldn't be a big deal if you couldn't get pregnant. But I really *do* want a baby! Marly, we're going to be parents! We're having a baby!" he said, his smile as big as the moon. He hugged her again, and Marly felt all the stress and anxiety of holding the secret in leave.

"One more secret," she said to him.

"What could be bigger than this?" he asked.

"It's a boy."

Marly knew that having a boy had been Jasper's dream. Sure, he would have been happy with a girl—any sex, really—as long as it was healthy. But he had talked forever about having a son to continue the family name.

Suddenly Jasper jumped up on the table, and Marly heard the crowd gasp.

"It's a boy!" he yelled, raising his glass in the air.

The entire room erupted in cheers.

18

"To a successful and eventful night!" Veronica said, raising her champagne flute into the air.

Sarah raised her glass and laughed along with Marly, Harper, Logan, and Raffe. The ball was over, and the cleaning crew was clearing everything up, but a few of them had remained after all of the other guests had left.

"Well, this was quite the night, wasn't it?" Gertie asked as she wheeled up beside Sarah. "We made almost a million dollars for the Kidney Foundation!"

"Gertie! That's great!" Sarah said, knowing that the goal had been set at half a million dollars. "What about Brenda? What did the police say?"

"Well, they wanted me to press charges, but I'm not going to. And before you say anything, dear, remember what I say. Everyone deserves a second chance. It seems Brenda is separated now, and she just focused on losing that cooking show contest and made that the root of her problems. She knows what she did was stupid. Besides, if she really was a horrible person, she would have let Kidney eat that soup."

"Good point," Sarah said.

"I'm taking her to the shelter tomorrow to help her pick a cat out. It'll do her some good. And I'm going to get her the name of a good therapist."

Meow!

Kidney appeared, as if to agree with Gertie, and jumped onto her lap, settling down for a snooze. Gertie petted the cat. "There you are! I was getting worried. Good thing you didn't get any of that soup."

"Yeah, good thing." Sarah reached over to pet Kidney. They'd looked for him after he'd run off, but he couldn't be found. Thankfully, he seemed no worse for the wear.

"Well, those two seem to be getting kind of cozy," Raffe said to Sarah and Gertie, nodding his head toward the next table over. Myrtle and Edward were nose deep in a crossword puzzle, laughing over something.

"If I didn't know better, I might think that

Edward has a crush on someone else now," Harper said.

"That would be fantastic!" Gertie laughed. Her phone rang with a call from Tanner, and she excused herself to answer it.

"Congratulations," Raffe said to Sarah, handing her his phone. She read the screen, which was Franz Durkin's review.

"Wow, that was fast. He must have written it on his way home in the Uber." Sarah continued to read it. Franz had given the food five stars, which he hardly ever did. Even at EightyEight, they had only received four stars.

"It's well deserved," Raffe said, leaning over and kissing Sarah.

She looked around the room. Gertie was holding her phone up and FaceTiming with Tanner, a smile on her face. Marly and Jasper were bent over Marly's phone, looking at baby clothes with TJ and Veronica. Myrtle and Edward were hunched over a crossword puzzle, their knees touching from sitting too close.

Sarah grabbed Raffe's hand, and he smiled at her. It looked like everything was going to turn out all right for everyone involved after all.

****

Join my email list and receive emails about my latest book releases - plus I'll send you a link to download one of my books for free!:
http://www.leighanndobbs.com/newsletter

Join my Facebook Readers group and get special content and the inside scoop on my books:
https://www.facebook.com/groups/ldobbsreaders

OTHER BOOKS IN THIS SERIES:

In Over Her Head (book 1)
Can't Stand the Heat (book 2)
What Goes Around Comes Around (book 3)
Careful What You Wish For (4)

ALSO BY LEIGHANN DOBBS

Contemporary Romance

***

Reluctant Romance

Sweet Romance (Written As Annie Dobbs)

Firefly Inn Series

***

Another Chance (Book 1)

Another Wish (Book 2)

Hometown Hearts Series

***

No Getting Over You (Book 1)

A Change of Heart (Book 2)

Cozy Mysteries

Lexy Baker
Cozy Mystery Series

* * *

Lexy Baker Cozy Mystery Series Boxed Set Vol 1 (Books 1-4)

Or buy the books separately:

Killer Cupcakes

Dying For Danish

Murder, Money and Marzipan

3 Bodies and a Biscotti

Brownies, Bodies & Bad Guys

Bake, Battle & Roll

Wedded Blintz

Scones, Skulls & Scams

Ice Cream Murder

Mummified Meringues

Brutal Brulee (Novella)

No Scone Unturned

Cream Puff Killer

Kate Diamond Mystery Adventures

***

Hidden Agemda (Book 1)

Ancient Hiss Story (Book 2)

Heist Society (Book 3)

Silver Hollow

Paranormal Cozy Mystery Series

***

A Spell of Trouble (Book 1)

Spell Disaster (Book 2)

Nothing to Croak About (Book 3)

Cry Wolf (Book 4)

Mooseamuck Island

Cozy Mystery Series

* * *

A Zen For Murder

A Crabby Killer

A Treacherous Treasure

Mystic Notch

Cat Cozy Mystery Series

* * *

Ghostly Paws

A Spirited Tail

A Mew To A Kill

Paws and Effect

Probable Paws

Blackmoore Sisters

Cozy Mystery Series

* * *

Dead Wrong

Dead & Buried

Dead Tide

Buried Secrets

Deadly Intentions

A Grave Mistake

Spell Found

Fatal Fortune

Hazel Martin Historical Mystery Series

***

Murder at Lowry House (book 1)

Murder by Misunderstanding (book 2)

Lady Katherine Regency Mysteries

***

An Invitation to Murder (Book 1)

The Baffling Burglaries of Bath (Book 2)

Sam Mason Mysteries

(As L. A. Dobbs)

***

Telling Lies (Book 1)

Keeping Secrets (Book 2)

Exposing Truths (Book 3)

Betraying Trust (Book 4)

Romantic Comedy

***

Corporate Chaos Series

In Over Her Head (book 1)

Can't Stand the Heat (book 2)

What Goes Around Comes Around (book 3)

Careful What You Wish For (4)

***

Sweetrock Sweet and Spicy Cowboy Romance

Some Like It Hot

Too Close For Comfort

Regency Romance

* * *

Scandals and Spies Series:

Kissing The Enemy

Deceiving the Duke

Tempting the Rival

Charming the Spy

Pursuing the Traitor

Captivating the Captain

The Unexpected Series:

An Unexpected Proposal

An Unexpected Passion

Dobbs Fancytales:

Dobbs Fancytales Boxed Set Collection

Western Historical Romance

***

Goldwater Creek Mail Order Brides:

Faith

American Mail Order Brides Series:

Chevonne: Bride of Oklahoma

Magical Romance with a Touch of Mystery

***

Something Magical

Curiously Enchanted

ROMANTIC SUSPENSE
WRITING AS LEE ANNE JONES:

***

The Rockford Security Series:

Deadly Betrayal (Book 1)

Fatal Games (Book 2)

Treacherous Seduction (Book 3)

Calculating Desires (Book 4)

Wicked Deception (Book 5)

ALSO BY LISA FENWICK

This Wasn't The Plan (What's the Plan? Series Book 1)

Backup Plan (What's the Plan? Series Book 2)

Exit Plan (What's the Plan? Series Book 3)

ABOUT LEIGHANN DOBBS

USA Today bestselling author, Leighann Dobbs, discovered her passion for writing after a twenty year career as a software engineer. She lives in New Hampshire with her husband Bruce, their trusty Chihuahua mix Mojo and beautiful rescue cat, Kitty. When she's not reading, gardening, making jewelry or selling antiques, she likes to write cozy mystery and historical romance books.

Her book "Dead Wrong" won the "Best Mystery Romance" award at the 2014 Indie Romance Convention.

Her book "Ghostly Paws" was the 2015 Chanticleer Mystery & Mayhem First Place category winner in the Animal Mystery category.

Find out about her latest books by signing up at:

http://www.leighanndobbs.com/newsletter

Connect with Leighann on Facebook
http://facebook.com/leighanndobbsbooks

Join her VIP readers group on Facebook:
https://www.facebook.com/groups/ldobbsreaders/

This is a work of fiction.

None of it is real. All names, places, and events are products of the author's imagination. Any resemblance to real names, places, or events are purely coincidental, and should not be construed as being real.

DISH BEST SERVED COLD

Copyright © 2020

Leighann Dobbs Publishing

http://www.leighanndobbs.com

All Rights Reserved.

No part of this work may be used or reproduced in any manner, except as allowable under "fair use," without the express written permission of the author.

❀ Created with Vellum

Printed in Great Britain
by Amazon